ABDUCTED IN THE KEYS
A LOGAN DODGE ADVENTURE

FLORIDA KEYS ADVENTURE SERIES
VOLUME 9

LOGAN DODGE ADVENTURES

Gold in the Keys
Hunted in the Keys
Revenge in the Keys
Betrayed in the Keys
Redemption in the Keys
Corruption in the Keys
Predator in the Keys
Legend in the Keys
Abducted in the Keys

Join the Adventure!
Sign up for my newsletter to receive updates on
upcoming books on my website:

matthewrief.com

PROLOGUE

Miami, Florida
August 2010

It was just after midnight. After checking one more time that the coast was clear, the girl slid open her window and dropped onto the grass below. She kept to the shadows. Moved quickly, but quietly. Across the knoll. Into a cluster of palm trees.

She stopped when she reached the road. The evening was silent, aside from a soft breeze through the overhead fronds and the beating of her heart.

Hard part's over, she thought.

She was fifteen. Tall and pretty. Long dark hair, high cheekbones, big hazel eyes, and a narrow waist. She looked more woman than girl.

She'd spent most of her life bouncing from foster home to foster home, and the occasional group home. She'd been living at St. Mary's for over a year, but it had felt like an eternity.

Time to pretend to be a normal teenager. At least for one night.

She stepped out from the trees, darted across the street, down a few blocks, then hopped onto a bus heading downtown. While riding, she thought about him.

William.

She'd met him two weeks earlier in an online chat room. He'd been sweet, flirty, and best of all, interested in her. He was also seventeen and had a car and a job.

And his profile picture.

She smiled as she pictured him.

Like a modern-day James Dean. The classy handsome bad boy look.

The bus's hydraulics hissed. The doors opened. She stepped out two blocks from their agreed-upon meeting place.

A restaurant she'd never heard of in a part of town she'd never been to. She tried to remember the name of it.

Something Italia.

Sounded fancy to her. And after, he said they could go see a movie. She couldn't remember the last time she'd been to a theater. Well over a year. Nothing but old movies played on a television that was deeper than it was wide ever since.

Maybe he'll buy us some popcorn. And soda.

Her excitement and anticipation rose with every step on the sidewalk. She looked around, keeping an eye out for something Italia.

The street was quiet. She spotted only three people and one car in five minutes of walking through the humid evening air.

She reached an intersection and turned left. Up ahead, she spotted a sign above a building with large glass windows and smiled.

Amore Dall'italia.

She strode over, stopped in front of the doors. They were closed.

Of course.

She wondered if William knew. Wondered if maybe the restaurant had recently changed their hours.

She knew she wasn't too late. She didn't own a cellphone or wear a watch, but she trusted her mental clock. She'd left at midnight, and the trip over had taken no longer than half an hour. Twelve thirty. That had been the agreed-upon time.

She stood and waited for a few minutes.

She looked down at her outfit. Skinny jeans. A blue tank top. Nothing posh, but they were the nicest clothes that she had.

Hopefully, William will think I look pretty.

She waited another minute. She strolled back and forth. Looked up, looked down, bit her lip a few times. Just as she wondered when the next bus would arrive, she heard footsteps on the sidewalk beside her. She turned and saw a tall guy wearing jeans and a white polo shirt.

He looked good. Styled hair and a chiseled jaw and a nice tan.

"Scarlett?" he said, his voice smooth as silk.

She nodded.

"Willi—"

"You come alone?" he added, cutting her off.

Another nod.

"Yeah, I…" She paused a moment, then glanced at the dark restaurant beside her. "They're closed."

William stepped in close. Flicked his cigarette into a street gutter. He looked and sounded much older than seventeen.

He reached out, grabbed her hand softly, and smiled.

"You look even better in person," he said. Before she could reply, he motioned behind him. "I know another place. It isn't far."

She smiled, and they held hands as he led the way. A big diesel truck grumbled by. Scarlett could hear music coming from a bar in the distance.

She was just about to ask him where they were going when he led her toward a dark alley.

"It's right on the other side," he assured her. "Best cheeseburgers in town. And they're open until two."

She followed him. A stray cat eyed them from beside a dumpster. She could barely see it by the light of the moon. The alley became darker the deeper they moved into it. It didn't look like it led anywhere except a dead end.

"William, this looks—"

She froze as an engine started up and a pair of bright headlights switched on just a few steps in front of her. She shielded her eyes and tried to squeal. But she couldn't. Something was blocking her mouth.

She trembled in fear as she realized what was happening. William had crept up, grabbed her from behind, and pressed his right hand over her mouth. He squeezed her so tight she could barely breathe.

Scarlett watched in terror as the van's side door slid open violently. Two guys dressed all in black climbed out and moved toward them. One had a sack in his hands. The other a coil of rope.

Her dread turned to anger. She struggled with everything she had. Bit down hard on William's fingers. Let out a shrill cry and elbowed him in the gut.

William groaned and cursed. Scarlett managed a single step out of there before the other two closed in. They grabbed her, smacked her over the head, then held her down.

Scarlett felt a sharp pinch, then felt woozy and passed out on the blacktop.

"The bitch," William said, eyeing his bloody fingers.

He reared back to kick Scarlett's unconscious body, but one of the other guys stopped him.

"No damaging the merchandise," the guy grumbled, holding William back. He motioned toward the van and added, "Get her loaded up with the other two. The three of them need to be ready for delivery tomorrow evening."

They carried Scarlett's limp body into the van. Then they climbed inside and slammed the door shut.

Within seconds they were on the main road, putting distance between themselves and the scene.

ONE

Florida Keys
The Next Day

This was it. The stage was set. Mano a mano. The moment of truth.

I gripped my weapon with both hands and homed in on my quarry. With my lungs throbbing, I narrowed my gaze, took aim, and pulled the trigger.

The stretched rubber tubing snapped free, launching the metal spear through the gin-clear tropical water. I watched as the three-pronged sharpened steel tip struck home. It sliced through the unsuspecting wahoo just between its dark left eye and pectoral fin. With little more than a twitch, my prey went motionless, and I reeled it in.

A clean kill.

I grabbed hold of the spear right where it entered flesh, and looked up. I finned smoothly for the surface, exhaled as I broke free, and took in a few quick, much-needed gulps of fresh sea air. Grabbing the wahoo by the meat of its tail fin, I raised its elongated blue-and-silver body up out of the water. I dug my other hand into its gills, steering clear of its razor-sharp teeth.

My wife, Angelina, stood against the transom of my 48 Baia Flash. Her smile was nearly as big as my own when she laid eyes on my catch.

"You couldn't have gotten a bigger one?" she said.

I laughed. Pulling off my mask, I let it hang around my neck.

"I'll try to do better next time," I joked as I kicked toward the stern.

She had her hands on her hips, her blond hair tied back, and was peering at me through a pair of aviator sunglasses. Wearing a turquoise bikini, her lean, tanned body glistened in the late afternoon sun.

"Wahoo!" Jack shouted when he surfaced beside me.

Shouting "Wahoo!" after surfacing with a speared wahoo was a tradition that Jack kept up religiously.

Jack Rubio was one of my best and oldest friends. A fourth-generation conch, Jack was the owner of Rubio Charters, a fishing and diving charter that had been catching the ocean's bounties and showing tourists the underwater world since the eighties. Jack was a few inches shorter than my six-two, with curly blond hair, a deep tan, and a wiry frame.

"We're gonna need to grab the scale for that one, bro," Jack said, enthusiastically.

He held up a black mesh bag and I counted three spiny-tailed lobsters stashed inside. He'd already caught his limit for the day, so now he was just trying to up the sizes.

"The bugs are hot this year," Jack added as he finned for the port-side gunwale and dropped the bag on the deck.

It was August 6. Opening day of lobster season. After four months of only being able to watch the crustaceans with watering mouths, the time of delicious reckoning had come. Like Christmas morning in the island chain.

I plopped my catch down on the swim platform, removed my mask and fins, and climbed up out of the water. Jack heaved over the gunwale while Ange stepped over the transom and helped me haul up the wahoo.

My happy yellow Lab, Atticus, ran down, whipping his tail against everything as he jumped into my arms and practically knocked me back into the water. I glanced at my dive watch and saw that I'd been under for just over three minutes. An eternity for a dog.

I grabbed his tennis ball and tossed it out over the water. Before it had even splashed, Atticus was on the focused hunt, diving into the water and swimming quickly. Ange handed me a towel and I dried off while Jack sorted through the lobster in the live well, tossing out a few of the smaller ones for a later time.

I stowed my gear, then took a quick picture with my fish before wrapping it in last week's edition of the *Keynoter* and putting it on ice in my big cooler. Pulling out my portable grill, we cooked up some of the lobster tails right on the water as the sun sank down toward the Gulf of Mexico.

Ange steamed up some vegetables in the galley and Jack whipped up a few rum runner cocktails. Once ready, we plated the food and ate it up on the bow while watching the sunset. The clouds covering much of the western sky had turned a deep shade of purple with glowing fringes. Streaks of rebellious light broke free at the shifting cracks, casting beams across the sky and twinkling like diamonds over the water.

My father had taught me years ago to always watch the sunset if you can. It's a good time to pause and reflect on the events of the day. Reminisce about the good stuff and learn from your mistakes.

After a string of rip-roaring adventures that had taken their toll on us physically and mentally, things had slowed down. I hadn't even fired my Sig Sauer P226 pistol since we'd taken down Valmira Gallani, an Albanian mafia leader who'd tried to kill us and take the Florentine Diamond for herself. That was last October. Nearly a year ago. Aside from a few trips down to Curacao in the Dutch Caribbean, Ange and I had spent all of 2010 in the Florida island chain.

I'd turned thirty-three in February. Ange and I had had our first anniversary in May. Most of my life had been characterized by action, travel, and more action. Always another bad guy. Always another fight. And though I enjoyed bringing justice upon the doorstep of those who deserved it, I'd be content spending the rest of my days right there on the boat, spearfishing, diving, and sucking the marrow out of life.

I kissed Ange on the cheek, then petted Atticus and took another savory bite of the buttered grilled lobster. Fresh seafood didn't get any fresher than that.

Just after the final rays of sun sank into the water, Jack's phone vibrated to life on the bow deck beside him. He answered the call, smiled, then turned to us.

"Lauren just got done with her charter," he said. "She's on her way to Conch Haven on Lower Sugarloaf to see the Wayward Suns. You two up for some live music?"

Lauren Sweetin had moved to Key West from Tennessee after divorcing her cheating husband two years ago. After the courageous change of scenery, she'd dived headfirst into the island lifestyle, buying a catamaran and starting her own snorkeling charter company.

She and Jack had been flirty with each other for a while and had finally made their relationship official a few months ago. I ragged on him that it was about time. Jack and Lauren were a match made in tropical heaven.

"I'll have to check my schedule, Jack," I said with a grin as I leaned back and took another swig of my rum runner.

"Schedule? What is this word?" Ange added.

"Count us in, sweetie," Jack said into his phone. "We'll see you there."

When we finished eating, we headed back down into the saloon, cleaned up a little, then I started up the Baia's twin 600-hp engines. Operating the windlass remotely, I brought the anchor up, then Jack secured the safety lanyard.

I eased forward on the throttles and brought us around to an easterly heading. Once on course, I glanced at the radar before bringing us up to the Baia's cruising speed of forty knots. I loved the feeling of bringing my boat up to speed, hearing the ocean crash against the bow, feeling the warm wind whip against my face whenever I rose up over the windscreen.

TWO

Twenty minutes later, I pulled us into an empty space on the dock in front of Conch Haven restaurant. After killing the engines and tying off, I dropped down into the main cabin and put on a pair of cargo shorts and a faded Rubio Charters tee shirt. Ange dressed in a black tank top and denim shorts, while Jack was content with his board shorts and tattered ball cap. I swear, the guy never takes those shorts off.

I fed Atticus, filled his water bowl, then cracked open a few of the windows so he wouldn't get too hot. After locking it up and engaging the security system that I'd installed myself after buying her over two years ago, we headed down the dock, following the sound of the music.

Conch Haven restaurant is a two-story, well-renovated local joint that's right on the water. To the south is a condominium complex, to the north an empty lot followed by a long stretch of abandoned wharves, docks, and structures that Jack told me used to be part of a sponge factory.

Lauren waved at us from the second level, her smile as big as they come.

"Come on up," she said enthusiastically over the sound of the band. "I saved the table, so first round's on you guys."

We walked along the sand that transitioned to a pinewood deck. There wasn't too much of a crowd, and it consisted mostly of locals. August isn't exactly the high tourist season in the Keys. With average highs of eighty-nine degrees and the threat of hurricanes, it's no wonder. But opening day of lobster season does bring down a throng of hungry, adventurous exterminators every year.

Heading up the stairs, we weaved through the tables and waitresses, reaching Lauren over by the edge. She'd picked a good spot, with a great view of the ocean as well as the band.

"You three save some lobster for the rest of us?" Lauren said before pulling Jack in for a kiss.

"The small ones," he said after catching a breath.

Lauren was pretty, with long auburn hair, tanned skin, and a voluptuous figure. She also had a personality that was an attractive blend of humor and intelligence. I'd liked her from our first meeting.

Having already eaten dinner, I decided on a Paradise Sunset beer when the waitress came over. Lauren had ordered a big plate of shrimp nachos that arrived just after we did, and snacking on the occasional cheesy tortilla chip filled what little room remained in my stomach.

I turned my attention to the section of deck that had been cleared for the band's stage. The Wayward Suns were a Florida band that toured primarily up and down the coasts, from Savannah to Key West. I hadn't heard them in a while and wasn't about to pass up an opportunity. I listened and bobbed my head as they sang of secret faraway beaches, old beach chairs, and crashing waves. The islander's idea of the land of milk and honey.

When they finished their song to impressive applause and cheers, the lead singer took a swig of his drink, then grabbed the mic. His name was Cole Daniels. I'd met him a few times and considered him a friend. He had long dreads, wore an orange bandana, and had a lanky physique. Placing his right hand over his eyes to shield them from the overhead lights, he scanned the crowd, then made eye contact with me.

He nodded to me, and I nodded back and bowed the neck of my beer slightly.

They cranked up a song I'd never heard before. It had a pretty good beat, their usual reggae and country music flair. I smiled once the lyrics started. It was about a bunch of rough biker types starting trouble at one of their performances. After a little too much cursing and tossing of cans, someone had given them what was coming to them.

I smiled.

That was the first night I'd heard the Wayward Suns back at Salty Pete's in Key West. It had been a good night, and aside from the bloody knuckles and the lucky punch to my shoulder, it had been a good fight too.

I smiled as they went into the chorus, then smiled bigger as I looked around the table. I hadn't been living in the islands as long as Jack or some of our other friends, but it felt more like home than anywhere I'd ever lived.

Jack and Lauren steered the conversation to their charter operations while we finished off the nachos and drank to the music. With the two of them eagerly engaged, Ange and I reminisced about our honeymoon.

"We should go back to Tahiti," she said with a wink. "I think we're due for a trip."

"Getting a little antsy?"

"Maybe. But don't get me wrong"—she nestled her head against my shoulder and directed her gaze to the band—"this isn't so bad either."

I nursed my way through two beers and, as the band took a break, slid out from the table and migrated toward the head. It was half past ten and the place was starting to heat up. When I managed to slide through the tables, chairs, patrons, and staff, I reached the restroom along the backside of the restaurant. To my surprise, there was a line. Apparently the place only had a single unisex bathroom.

I shook my head.

Gonna have to harp on the owner that this won't fly, I thought.

I made an about-face, pushed out a squeaky door, then headed downstairs. There were a few people mingling in the parking lot and a couple holding hands out on the dock. With the sun good and gone, the waning crescent moon cast a small silvery glow over the beach and calm waters of Sugarloaf Sound.

I caught a whiff of tobacco smoke, then slapped the top of my left forearm. With the relative cool of the evening came the island chain's most unwelcome residents: mosquitoes. The ocean breeze usually helped keep them at bay, but tonight the weather was calmer than an opium den.

17

My bladder reminded me of my mission. I made my way up the beach, heading north toward a cluster of trees. When I was out of sight, I unzipped and let out a deep breath as I relieved myself. Once done, I zipped my shorts back up and tightened the belt.

Looking out over the water, I closed my eyes and took in an enjoyable breath of fresh sea air. Just as I began to turn back around, something caught my eye. A small flash of light. It came from farther up the beach, near the abandoned structures and docks.

I stared in the direction where I thought I'd seen the light for a few seconds.

How much did I drink?

Just the two beers, but I'd had the rum runner on the boat. For a former Navy sailor, that's just getting your feet wet.

Maybe it was nothing. Maybe I'm just seeing things.

I was just about to turn back once more when I saw it again. This time it was clear. No mistaking. No blaming it on mind games. Inside the middle structure along the water, there was a small flash that shone through what remained of a row of broken dirty windows. And it was followed moments after by another flash.

I moved down the beach instinctively while keeping my eyes on the structure. There was nobody around, and it was a decent walk from the restaurant or the nearest road.

Most likely? I figured it was a hot and heavy couple about to cross off a fantasy from their list. An old, dirty, smelly, rundown building wasn't near the top of mine, but to each their own.

Regardless, I wanted to make sure.

Curiosity killed the cat, but satisfaction brought it

back.

I moved closer. Seeing the light appear near the ocean-facing end of the structure, where it opened up to the old wharf, I leaned against a thick support beam. From their angle, I'd be in the moon's shadow and nearly impossible to see.

I stood still and waited.

I'd been in the Keys for over a year without fighting anyone. Not that I'd gone looking for a fight since my days as a mercenary, but trouble tended to find me more often than not. It was likely I was making more of it than it was. Maybe I was just throwing rocks in the pond then and wondering where the waves had come from.

But I had a feeling, a good old-fashioned hunch. And over the years I'd learned to trust my instincts. They'd saved me more times than I could count.

I watched with a narrowed gaze as the light suddenly vanished. Seconds later, a dark figure appeared on the wharf. Two more followed, then a couple more. I counted five in all. Hard to tell in the dark and so far away, but it looked like two men and three women.

Strange.

They weren't talking. Weren't joking and laughing like you would expect friends to do while venturing off late at night.

When they moved onto one of the docks, I knew that something was very wrong. The three women weren't walking with the two guys. They were being prodded by them. Their arms were bound at the wrists, and as a streak of the moon's glow broke between the clouds, I saw that they each had sacks tied over their heads.

THREE

I narrowed my gaze, watching intently as the two men forced the women down the dock. My mind went to work instantly, running over scenarios and likely outcomes.

I had no way of knowing who any of them were. Out-of-towners, no doubt. But one thing was clear: the three women weren't there of their own free will.

I'd witnessed sex traffickers in action before, but this was my first time seeing it stateside. It didn't take a genius to surmise what these guys would do to them. Drugs, abuse, more drugs. Then a lifetime of forced sex and beatings until they either died or killed themselves. Makes me sick to my stomach. Few things boil my blood faster and with such intensity as this.

Just as the group was about to reach the end of the dock, I made my move. Quietly, I crept out from along the support beam and moved for the cover of a small shed up on the wharf. The old planks groaned and creaked, so I kept my steps as light and smooth as possible. Reaching the other side of the shed, I peeked around the corner.

The group had made it to the end of the dock. One of the guys had a cellphone pressed to his ear, its faint glow flashing like a distant lighthouse with his movements. I couldn't hear what he was saying, but I didn't need to. He was calling in to one of his lowlife buddies for a pickup.

A few seconds later, he pressed a button on the phone and dropped it into his front pocket. He said something to the other guy that I couldn't hear, then lit up a cigarette. There was still about a hundred yards of beach and dock between us. I needed to get closer, but there wasn't much in the way of cover, and the soft waves would do little to muffle my movements.

Suddenly, the quiet, eerie scene woke to life as one of the girls cried out. It was a high-pitched cry of panic and desperation.

The sound was silenced as abruptly as it had started, with one of the guys knocking the woman across the face with a strong backhand. I watched as she stumbled and fell hard to the old planks, her brave cries transitioning to groans of pain.

"Shut the hell up!" one of the guys hissed.

I used the distraction to move in. Keeping low, I strode across an open section of beach and dropped down at the base of the dock. From there, I could see the group clearly.

A guy bent down, grabbed the prone woman, and jerked her violently to her feet.

"You make another sound and I'll blow your head off," the guy said, pulling her close and causing her to gasp for air as he squeezed a hand around her neck.

The guy holding her was big. He looked a little taller than my six foot two and probably had thirty pounds on me. The other guy was shorter and leaner. He had styled hair and was dressed much better than the big guy. Both were hard and rough. This clearly wasn't their first time transporting kidnapped women.

The thought of going for help or staying out of it altogether never entered my mind. These were innocent young girls. They were somebody's daughters. Somebody somewhere was worried sick and searching frantically for them. Besides, it was two against one. I'd never had a problem with those kinds of odds.

I sized up my adversaries once more. Even up closer, I couldn't see any visible weapons, but I had no doubt that they were both carrying.

I didn't want to waste any more time. Whoever they'd just called was motoring their way, and I doubted they'd have to wait long.

I could pop up and just shoot the guys from there. I was only about fifty feet away. Closer than a pitcher to home plate. I trusted my aim. With my Sig I could knock a cap off a bottle from that distance nine times out of ten. I'd fired the special forces handgun thousands of times in my life. But with the three girls so close, I couldn't risk any of them moving into a bullet's path.

I looked down at the dock and thought over my options. If I wasn't going to shoot them, I needed to get close to them without drawing too much suspicion.

My eyes settled on an object pinned against the bottom of the dock. I leaned in closer and realized what it was. Somebody had abandoned an old rod and reel. I picked it up. The bail was so rusted it couldn't move. The rod was missing more guides than it had, and the line was tangled. But in the dark and the heat of the moment, I doubted either of the guys would notice. It was as good of a cover as I was going to get.

I listened for a few seconds. All I could hear was the soft lapping waves, the squawking of a few distant gulls, and the quiet whimpers of the shaking women. One of the guys stood at the end, taking intermittent drags of his cigarette. The other leaned against an old brace.

Holding the fishing pole, I rose to my feet.

Showtime.

I played the part of the slightly intoxicated late-night fisherman as best I could. I walked with heavy steps on the dock, swaying every now and then, and hummed "what do you do with a drunken sailor" just loud enough for them to hear me.

The two guys were startled and strode in front of the three girls.

"What the hell are you doing here, asshole?" the big guy said.

He had a Spanish accent. It was hard and stern. He was trying to scare me off.

I froze in place and stared stupidly into the darkness, shifting my head from side to side as if that would help me get a better look.

"Just going after the midnight bite," I said nonchalantly. I started walking again and directed my gaze out over the water. "Snapper run right through here to feed off the—"

"Shut the hell up and take a hike, buddy," the pretty boy said with a laugh. "The dock's closed."

He was laughing. That was good. It meant that he had no idea that he was about to feel some serious

23

pain.

I ignored him and kept moving, stopping along the left side and fidgeting with the reel. I was within ten feet of the two guys and was hoping they'd take the bait and close in. They did.

"Hey, asshole," the big guy snarled as he strode toward me with heavy steps. "Are you deaf? The dock's closed. Now get out of here before we make you."

I nodded, acting as unaffected as possible.

"Yep, great night for fishin'," I said, slurring my words a little and clicking the bail loose.

"Hey," Big Guy said, striding toward me. "Move the fuck out!"

He grabbed my right wrist. It was a strong overhand grip. As he did, I caught a gleam of metal peeking out from the right side of his waistband. I only needed a quick glance to realize that it was the familiar shape of a handgun grip.

The second guy moved in right behind the big one. They were both close now, well within striking distance. My little charade had done its job.

"You've got three seconds," Big Guy said, his temper boiling over like a forgotten teakettle. "One… two…"

Before he could say three, I dropped the reel and spun around. As fast as I could, I twisted my right hand free of his grasp and grabbed hold of his wrist. Bending my knees, I dropped down and pulled him over my body. His arm broke in more than one place, and he could only yell out as his body flew through the air and crashed so hard onto the old dock that his weight shattered a few planks. With my other hand grabbing my dive knife, I stabbed it straight through the big guy's heart.

In the blink of an eye, he was gone.

I turned to engage the second guy. Just as we locked eyes, he reached for his weapon. But before he could pull it free, I struck him with a snapping side kick to the throat. I felt the heel of my right foot crunch his trachea, causing his head to snap forward and air to gasp from his lungs. He placed both hands around his neck, struggling hard to breathe as he fell hard to the dock.

I strode over and held him down while relieving him of his handgun and a Ka-Bar sheathed to his belt. Once his weapons splashed in the water, I grabbed his left shin and broke his leg like I was snapping a thick branch for firewood.

He yelled out as loud as he could given his throat damage and rolled back and forth. He tried to curse me out, but the words were barely audible. I knelt down, slid up his tee shirt, and tightened it forcefully around his mouth to keep him quiet.

With the big guy dead and the other guy down for the count, I turned my attention to the women. They cried and stepped away during the fight, nearly to the opposite edge of the dock. I took in a few breaths to calm myself while moving toward them.

"It's alright," I said, sounding as reassuring as possible. "Your two captors are down. There's no need to be scared anymore."

I grabbed the fabric sack tied over the closest one's face. She jerked back, but I still managed to loosen it enough to pull it off. Then I untied the other two's hoods as well. I grabbed one of the thug's flashlights and quickly looked them over to make sure they were alright.

All three of them pretty and thin young women. Two were blond with blue eyes, the third

25

brunette with hazel eyes. The dark-haired girl looked younger than the other two, though it was hard to tell for sure since she was taller. Maybe sixteen if I had to guess while the two blond girls looked to be in their late teens or early twenties.

"Who… who are you?" one of the blond girls asked after I removed their gags.

"My name is Logan Dodge," I said. "I was just down the beach and spotted you guys."

I grabbed my cellphone and quickly punched in a speed dial number.

"Ange, it's me," I said.

I asked where she was and she replied that she was in the parking lot wondering where I'd disappeared to.

"It's alright," I said.

I told her what had happened and instructed her to call the police and meet me up the beach. Just as I hung up and slid the phone back into my front pocket, the dark-haired girl ran over and started kicking the injured pretty boy thug. She yelled at him in anger while he grunted and groaned in pain. I stepped over, grabbed hold of her and pulled her away.

"He'll get what's coming to him, don't worry," I said.

"He deserves to die and rot in hell for what he does!" she fired back.

She was breathing heavily, her big eyes bulging out from her face. She looked like she hadn't eaten or slept in a while, and her clothes were dirty.

I rounded the three of them up and pointed toward the beach.

"I'll take care of them," I said. "Don't worry, this isn't the first bad guy I've dealt with. My wife's on her way and we'll get you safely out of here."

I could already see Ange's silhouette. She was moving quickly along the shoreline and would reach the dock in less than a minute.

Turning around, I heard the unmistakable sound of an outboard far out over the dark water.

Shit.

I snatched my Sig from its holster.

"Get to the beach," I said.

Just as the words left my lips, the night air was ripped to shreds by automatic gunfire.

The three girls dropped to the ground in an instant. Bullets splintered the dock planks around us. I kept the girls at my back and opened fire, sending a succession of bullets straight for the rapidly approaching boat. I heard a few rounds strike the white fiberglass-hulled craft, heard a guy yell out.

I couldn't see Ange, but I heard her firing from the shoreline as well. The automatic gunfire stopped suddenly. The boat's motor moaned, and the pilot performed a sharp 360-degree turn that nearly caused it to flip over. I fired off a few more rounds, aiming for the engine, then lowered my Sig.

"Who the hell was that?" Ange called out from the beach.

I kept my Sig raised, waiting a few more seconds to make sure the pilot didn't change his mind and about-face back toward us. The engine groaned far out over the water, getting quieter and quieter before eventually silencing completely.

With the immediate threat gone, I holstered my Sig. Ange reached us and knelt down right away to check on the girls.

"Get them out of here," I told her, kissing her on the forehead as I moved past.

"Where are you going?" she said, looking back

over her shoulder.

"To try to answer your question."

If whoever was piloting that boat thought they'd gotten off easy, they were gravely mistaken.

FOUR

I took off down the dock and reached the sandy shoreline in seconds. Jack was racing down the beach, gripping his compact Desert Eagle with two hands.

"What the hell's going on, bro?" he said through gasps for air.

"Sex traffickers," I said.

He stopped abruptly, shifting his gaze from me to the dock. I didn't slow as I approached him. I wasn't sprinting, but I was close to it.

"Girls are fine," I added. "One of the kidnappers got away on a center-console."

That was all it took for my beach bum friend to holster his Desert Eagle and run alongside me toward the parking lot. Jack wasn't a trained warrior, but he'd always been able to carry himself well and handle a weapon. We'd gotten into a handful of scrapes in our time. He was a good man to have at your side when shit hit the fan.

We reached the parking lot quickly and weaved through a few rows of cars to the small dock where the Baia was tied off. A large group of people had exited the restaurant and were standing around, wondering what all the commotion was about. Even with the Wayward Suns blaring out their island tunes, a storm of repetitive gunfire would have caught most everyone's attention.

I launched myself over the Baia's port gunwale and into the cockpit. Flipping up the keypad for the security system, I punched in the four-digit code, inserted the key into the ignition, then twisted. I looked over my shoulder as the engines gurgled to life. Jack already had the stern and bow lines untied. He gave me a quick thumbs-up before jumping onto the sunbed and quickly coiling the lines.

Less than thirty seconds after jumping aboard, I shoved the throttle forward. The engines roared and the propellers churned up a massive white-bubbled wake. We cleared the end of the dock in a blink and accelerated into the dark channel. The Baia's bow rose high out of the water. For a moment I couldn't see anything, then the bow splashed back down as we came up on plane.

Thirty knots. Forty, then the max speed of fifty. I turned the helm slightly to the right, heading in the direction where the center-console had disappeared. I scanned back and forth between the dark water surrounding us and the instruments. Depth there wasn't an issue. I'd boated there many times before and knew the shallowest portions of the channel were well deeper than the Baia's three-foot draft. The radar captured most of my attention. I kept my eye out for echoes, wanting to avoid collisions and to spot our running quarry.

Jack appeared from below deck with my backpack slung over his shoulder. Balancing himself with ease as we throbbed up and down at full speed, he reached inside and grabbed my night vision monocular. He quickly powered it on and peered at the horizon ahead of us.

Based on the pilot's trajectory, I assumed that he'd head north for the Gulf. I eased back on the throttles a little and cut through a channel beside Dreguez Key, heading up into Turkey Basin.

The Gulf side of the Keys can be a nightmare to navigate at night, especially at our current speed. Thousands of tiny islands litter the landscape, along with shallow reefs, cuts, and channels. Fortunately we both knew the area well, and I had my side-scan sonar up and running, so I'd at least have a quick heads-up if I was heading for danger.

The tropical evening air whipped past us as we stared forward. Glowing moonlight cast down over the water, allowing me to see the dark outlines of islands. We were nearing the day's second high tide, which made piloting a little easier.

The only other boat we'd seen out on the water was a pontoon cruiser back when we'd motored into Upper Sugarloaf Sound. It was nearly midnight. Not a lot of pleasure boaters cruised about that late, even on a Friday.

Hoping our quarry hadn't turned off course, I continued us into Turkey Basin. When we were halfway across the four-mile-long body of water, Jack froze and zoomed in with the night vision monocular.

"Got a bead on somebody," he said over the Baia's roaring engines. "White hull, maybe twenty-three feet long with a closed bow."

"That's them."

31

I hadn't gotten a great look back from the dock, but the size and color checked out.

Jack lowered the monocular and added, "They're heading north for the Barracuda Keys. Hauling ass for that small of a boat, bro. Gotta be nearly forty knots."

"How far off are they?"

I could see a glowing wake far ahead but couldn't gauge the distance.

"A mile," he fired back right away.

Jack had a scary ability to judge distances in the islands. Even in the dark, I'd bet a case of Paradise Sunsets that he was close to the mark.

I kept the throttles full and my eyes scanning back and forth between my instruments and the horizon. I managed to close in on them just as we reached the Barracudas. They motored into a narrow cut that was only a few feet deep. I chose a deeper channel just a hundred yards to the west.

"Take the helm, Jack," I shouted just as we were about to break out from the channel into the lower part of the Gulf.

He took over, and I moved downstairs, through the galley, and into the main cabin. Making quick work of my safe, I grabbed my M4 carbine assault rifle along with an extra thirty-round magazine. Back up on deck, I stabilized myself and took aim over the port side of the windscreen.

If this guy didn't know we were there, he would soon. I wanted to be the first to strike. I wanted them to know for certain that their bad night wasn't over yet. That we weren't the type to back down or let evil men slip away without doing everything we could to stop them.

I debated opening fire, but we were still a good distance away. Also, we were clear of the islands, so they had nowhere to hide. In the open waters of the Gulf, we could quickly close the gap and take them down.

"I'm picking up something on radar," Jack said, catching my attention.

I lowered my monocular and stepped over to the cockpit.

"It's a ship, and it's heading west," he added.

I looked down at the radar screen and spotted the echo right away.

"It's huge," I said.

I had to rub my eyes a few times, unable to believe what I was seeing. The object being shown on the screen had to be around three hundred feet long.

I peered through my monocular over the starboard bow. After a few seconds, I saw it: the massive silhouette of a freighter thundering west. At our current rates of speed and trajectories, it would cut directly in front of us in just a few minutes.

Wanting to try and stop the traffickers before we reached the freighter, I pocketed my monocular and gripped my M4 with both hands. I rose up over the windscreen and took aim. I fired off a few rounds as best I could. Both our boats were bouncing, and we were far off, but I managed to pepper a few rounds into the transom.

I let go of the trigger and grabbed my night vision monocular. Focusing on the boat, I could see two guys scrambling aboard and laying low for cover. They were still about a hundred yards off.

One of them grabbed what looked like a rifle, so I opened fire again. Both guys hit the deck before they could retaliate. It looked like I hit one of them, but I emptied the magazine just to be sure, filling their boat's hull and inner deck with lead.

"They're done for now, bro," Jack said.

He was right. If they weren't dead already from my barrage, their boat would be dead in the water at any second.

Suddenly, a massive beam of bright light shined into my eyes. I lowered my M4 and raised my right hand to shield my face. I dropped down to the deck, trying to adjust my eyes that couldn't see anything except blurry flashes. I managed to catch a glimpse over the windscreen. To my surprise, the light wasn't coming from the boat we were chasing. It was coming from high up on the deck of the passing freighter.

"Dammit," Jack said.

Unable to see as well, he eased back on the throttles.

Our gunshots must have spooked them. The captain and crew must have expected the worst and assumed that we were the bad guys.

"Get them on the radio," I said. "Tell them what's going on."

The last thing I wanted was for the guys we were chasing to engage the freighter and hurt any of their crewmembers.

I set my M4 on the half-moon seat beside me and slowly rose to my feet. There were two spotlights on us now, both coming from different parts of the freighter. Surprisingly, the massive cargo vessel hadn't slowed. It was still cutting through the water at what I assumed was its max speed.

Due to the bright lights, I could make out little on the freighter's deck. A few solid black figures and an apparent buzz of activity. To my astonishment, they didn't say anything through a megaphone.

Jack idled the engines as the massive freighter blazed by a few hundred yards ahead of us. It cut through the water between us and the boat we were pursuing, causing it to vanish behind a curtain of dark hull and stacks of shipping containers. The freighter appeared barely laden, riding high above the water.

The spotlights stayed on us as we waited patiently. Not able to get ahold of them on the radio, I held my empty hands in the air, trying to let them know that we weren't a threat. Not to them anyway.

It took less than half a minute for the ship to pass. I tried to look out over the water, but with the beams of light still blazing relentlessly in our eyes, I couldn't see a thing. Finally, the big ship gave a loud blare of its horn, then the lights switched off in an instant.

I rubbed my eyes and looked out over the water. Grabbing my monocular, I climbed up onto the bow and peered through the lenses to spot where our quarry was. I'd predicted their position based on their previous trajectory, but the boat wasn't there. It wasn't anywhere.

I called out to Jack. Looking over my shoulder, I saw the same blank *what the hell* expression that I knew was plastered all over my face.

FIVE

Jack tried again to contact the freighter. I scanned through the night vision monocular at the massive trail of white bubbles. There was a chance that the boat had been hit, that it had been too slow to clear the bow of the massive ship and had been smashed to pieces. But I knew that wasn't the case. We'd have heard the collision. No, the boat was gone, which meant that it was motoring along the starboard side of the freighter, using it for cover.

We remained idle and watched as the freighter grumbled away. We didn't have much of a choice. The spotlights weren't exactly a warm welcome. After years of fighting, I could spot the dark outline of firearms from far away. And there were guys with rifles on the deck of the freighter, as was expected, to protect the cargo. If we motored up there, they could very well open fire on us. It wasn't worth the risk.

After the fifth failed attempt at various frequencies

to contact the freighter, we called the Coast Guard. We needed both them and the freighter's crew to know what they were up against. We told the guy on the line everything we knew. We told them there were armed hostiles in the Gulf. We told them they were motoring along the starboard side of a freighter that was heading west. And we gave them the freighter's name: *Lady Delilah*.

By the time we ended the call, the freighter was a dark speck on the western horizon.

"They're probably gonna send a cutter out to the freighter," I said. I glanced over at Jack, who was staring silently out over the water. "Everything alright?"

He glanced at me and blinked a few times.

"Yeah."

His voice wasn't very convincing, so I raised my eyebrows at him.

"It's just, we've chased down our share of criminals on open water, and how many times have we failed to reel them in?"

He was right. When it came to boat chases, we had a pretty good track record.

"Not since last summer," I said. "In the Everglades."

One of the Harlan brothers had managed to get away from us in his airboat. Well, more like our boats collided and he swam off. But we managed to track down the notorious serial killer in the end, as well as his two murderer brothers.

"Something feels wrong," Jack added. "That's all."

I nodded. Something did feel wrong. Those guys had been motoring into the open water of the Gulf with us closing in right on their tail. They'd been done for. And then a ship had come in at full speed. It was bizarre seeing a freighter in that part of the Gulf. We were far off from any of the standard nearby shipping lanes. Then there was the timing. It was perfect. Things rarely go perfectly in life, and when they do, they're almost always methodically planned that way.

"They haven't gotten away yet," I said, trying to be a little more positive. "They've got nowhere to go, and the Guard will close in and do their thing."

I grabbed my M4 and moved down into the galley. Atticus was sprawled out on the dinette half-moon cushion. He stirred and jumped down to the deck when he saw me.

"Only you can nap through a firefight, boy," I said, petting him behind the ears.

I stowed my M4, then moved back topside and grabbed my satellite phone from my bag. With the Guard notified, Ange was my next call. She and the three girls were crammed in Lauren's Suzuki Samurai. They were almost to Stock Island and would reach the Lower Keys Medical Center in less than five minutes. It was the smart move on Ange's part. Though all three women appeared to be in decent health, aside from a few scratches and bruises, they needed to see a doctor. They'd most certainly been drugged with who knew what.

"Any problems taking down the runner?" she asked.

"We had a complication."

She went silent a moment. "What happened?"

"I'll tell you at the hospital. We're a few miles north of Snipe Point."

As we spoke, I put my destination into my digital chart plotter.

"Twenty minutes," Jack said behind me.

Sure enough, the program brought up my route. The time of the trip was listed as seventeen minutes if we maintained the Baia's cruising speed.

"It's gonna take time to get from the dock to the hospital," Jack said, defending the slight discrepancy.

Sometimes it almost scared me how well Jack knew the islands and boats. Though he probably wouldn't score too high on many generic standardized tests, he was a genius in what he specialized in.

"We'll be there in twenty," I told Ange, then we hung up.

It was just after midnight when we eased up to the dock in front of Florida Keys Community College. The college is right across the street from the hospital and is the closest place to tie off. A good friend of ours, Professor Frank Murchison, teaches there and is also a board member. He allows us free use of the dock.

After killing the engines, I locked up. I still had the saloon windows open for Atticus and his water bowl out. He'd have no problem falling right to sleep from the gentle rocking inside the cove.

As I stepped onto the dock, I noticed Jack hunched over the side of the Baia. He was loosening the stern line and, looking forward, I saw that he'd already untied the bow line.

"I'll take her back to the marina," he said. "That way you can head straight home after. I'll bring your truck back. You know I'm not big on hospitals anyway."

I nodded and handed him the keys to the Baia and my Tacoma. He started up the engines and I shoved him off.

I moved across the campus, through the parking

lot, and across College Road to the hospital. I spotted Lauren's Sammy in one of the first parking spots beside the emergency room entrance. The cool rush of air conditioning felt good as I passed through the double set of sliding glass doors. Being so late, the waiting area was empty, aside from a middle-aged black woman sitting behind the counter. She directed me down the hall, and I met up with Ange in a smaller secondary waiting area.

She was sitting in a green padded chair. Upon seeing me approach, she came to her feet and walked over. Her eyes examined me from head to toe before she wrapped her arms around me.

"What happened?" she asked.

"Not exactly sure. We chased the boat up into the Gulf. Had a good bead on 'em. Then a freighter came in, cruised between us, and the boat disappeared."

"Any word from the freighter's crew?"

"We weren't able to contact them. The only message they sent was via a pair of spotlights. But we called the Guard and they said they were sending a cutter." I looked around the small waiting area. "How are the girls?"

We let go of each other. She wasn't her usual self. Her face was stone serious. Her eyes thin. The bridge of her nose rippled. Ange had a list of things that really put her over the edge. Young women getting taken advantage of was right at the top.

"As good as can be expected," she replied after a moment of thought. "Lauren and I got to talking with them on the drive here."

She motioned down the hall. I turned and saw Lauren walking our way carrying two small paper cups filled with steaming coffee. I greeted her as she handed Ange one of the coffees and we stood beside

40

the doorway.

"What did they tell you?" I asked.

"The older blond girl did most of the talking," Ange said. "She and the other blond girl are from Miami. They're college students and had been spending a summer weekend with friends. All they could remember was that they'd been spending a night on the town barhopping when a group of guys grabbed them both and threw them into a van. Before they knew it, they were unconscious and woke up the next day with blindfolds on."

"They say how long they were held hostage?"

"They guessed just a day," Ange replied. "But they didn't know for sure. They said they'd been drugged multiple times."

I fell silent for a moment, thinking everything through.

"What about the third girl?" I asked. "The younger one?"

Ange shook her head. "She hasn't said a word. I picked up a few burgers on the drive over, assuming they'd be starving. The other two ate like it was their last meal, but she only had a few bites."

Lauren pointed me in the direction of the coffee, and I headed over and filled up a cup. The warm caffeinated beverage felt good. It had been a long day, and the adrenaline from the fight and subsequent chase was starting to wear off.

The three of us sat in the small waiting area for a few minutes before the ER doctor stepped out. He told us that they all had drugs in their systems and were suffering from shock. But he added that they'd be alright. The three of them would stay there overnight and the hospital would contact their families and child protective services the following

41

morning.

We were able to meet with the three girls in the other room. They were still shaken up, but Ange getting them food and their being in a hospital caused them to relax a little. The two blond women thanked me, but the younger girl didn't say a word. She just walked over, wrapped her arms around my waist, and buried her head in my chest.

Her subtle but powerful action choked me up a little. It choked up Ange as well.

"What happens to me now?" she said after a few seconds, speaking for the first time.

Her voice was soft and innocent. She sniffled and loosened her grip slightly.

"Now you get to go home," I said. "Doc says you'll spend the night here, then they'll contact your families."

She burrowed her head deeper, then brought it back. A few tears streaked down her cheek and she wiped them away with her hands. Her eyes were watery as she looked up at me. We made eye contact for a brief second. She was a beautiful young girl, with vibrant hazel eyes, a few freckles around her nose, and long dark hair. I imagined her getting all dressed up for prom or something. She was probably a popular girl, and was probably about as accustomed to this kind of situation as a fish was to dry land.

After a quick moment, she turned away and hunched over. I stepped toward her, but she held up a hand while keeping the other pressed to her mouth. It took a few seconds for it to click in my mind. She wasn't wailing, she was about to hurl.

"Bathroom?" she said, looking up toward the doctor.

The nurse came over and ushered her through the

door that led out into the hall.

"That normal?" Ange said, looking at the doctor.

He nodded.

"Traumatizing events affect people differently," he said in an English accent. "But I'll take another look at her once she's done."

We said goodbye to the two other girls, then headed for the lobby. The double sliding glass doors of the main entrance slid open one at a time, and a police officer walked in. I recognized her instantly as Jane Verona. Jane had been Key West's sheriff for just over a year. What had started out as a temporary replacement after the murder of the previous sheriff, Charles Wilkes, had been made permanent by a vote not long after.

A go-getter, Jane was tough as nails and a natural leader. Being a Latina and also being a hard-nosed woman in a line of work dominated by men, she gave off a strong Michelle Rodriguez vibe.

She gave us the rundown. The dead guy on the dock was taken to the Monroe County Medical Examiner in Marathon. The guy whose leg I'd cracked to pieces was taken into custody for questioning.

A few other cops arrived as well as a detective, and they took our statements as well as the girls'. Thanks to Jane, we only had to be there for a little over half an hour. Just as she gave us the all good, Jack flip-flopped through the main entrance.

Before we took off, Jane walked over to us and told us to hold on a second.

"I just got off the phone with LT Saunders of the Coast Guard," she said. "He said they're almost finished inspecting the freighter. Looks like it's clean. And the crew only remembers your boat, apparently.

They don't remember seeing another boat."

I shook my head, not able to believe what I was hearing.

That's impossible. The boat disappeared behind the massive ship. There's no way that the crew didn't at least see what happened to it.

I wanted to tell Jane that, but it'd been a long day. I made a quick mental note instead.

Call LT Saunders in the morning and figure out what happened.

As much as I wanted to get back out on the water bright and early for round two of lobster roundup, it looked like it would have to wait. I had more important things on the agenda. There was a boat with two armed sex traffickers somewhere near the Keys, and apparently, by some miracle, Jack and I were the only ones who'd seen them.

SIX

Earlier That Evening

The three-hundred-foot long freighter cut through the water at twenty-six knots. Two crewmembers gathered at the starboard railing and fired up the ship's boat recovery system at the order of their captain. Once powered on, they swung the massive boom out over the water and quickly lowered the slings.

A radio clipped to one of their waists crackled to life.

"Are you in position and ready?" a stern, hard voice asked through the speaker.

"Yes, sir," he replied.

"The target will be there soon. Stand by to submerge."

The two crewmembers watched as a twenty-three-foot Grady-White flew into view around the bow of the freighter. The small craft was nearly struck and smashed to pieces by the steel monster, clearing the bow by less than a hundred feet.

The crewmembers lowered the slings the rest of the way. They were wide and weighted, causing them to sink deep enough into the water for the boat to be captured. The unique design of the advanced retrieval system allowed the ship to catch and hoist a boat while moving.

The boat motored around then accelerated into the sling from behind. Once in place, the pilot gave a thumbs-up and the operators raised them out of the rushing water. The mechanical components hummed along, raising the boat up alongside the main deck. The small boat was in bad shape. The stern was riddled with bullet holes, the windscreen shattered.

The crewmembers helped the two passengers onto the deck. One was severely injured and immediately carried inside. The remaining passenger, a tall, wide-shouldered guy, stood frozen for a few seconds. The events of the evening piled up and hit him suddenly like a ton of bricks.

Who the hell were those guys? he thought. *And how did this happen?*

The captain of the cargo ship, a lean man in his fifties with gray hair and a permanently focused brow, strode along the deck toward the commotion.

"What the hell happened, Flynn?" he barked. "Where are the girls?"

"Those assholes happened," Flynn replied in a strong Australian accent. "They took them. We barely made it out with our lives." He paused a moment, looking flustered, then stepped toward the port side. "Where are they? Are they still approaching?"

"Don't worry," the captain said, stopping him with

a firm hand. "Our spotlights scared them off. Besides, they are the least of your worries now." He handed the Aussie a sat phone. "Time to call your boss and explain to him what happened."

Flynn grabbed the phone reluctantly. As he stepped toward the railing to make a call and break the bad news, he heard the captain give another order to his nearby crew.

"Hide the boat in this empty container," he said. "I expect visitors tonight after that engagement."

He'd been having a good day until the snatch team had decided to fuck up their evening. Aside from the hassle of dealing with the Coast Guard, who'd undoubtedly be sent to inspect their ship, he didn't much care. He'd be paid either way. He'd held up his end of the bargain. If anyone was going to pay for what had happened, it would be the guys who hadn't done their simple job.

The captain stomped off toward the bridge, and Flynn dialed the number. As he listened to the rhythmic ringing sound, he wished he'd been the one who'd been shot.

Then I wouldn't have to be the one to break the news.

"This better be good, Sergei," a commanding Hispanic voice answered.

"Boss, it's me," Flynn said, his voice shaky.

"Flynn? What the hell are you calling me for? You guys on your way here?"

Flynn bit hard, then flared his nostrils.

Here goes nothing.

"We're on the ship, but there was a problem at the pickup." He paused a moment; he could almost feel his boss's anger through the phone. "We didn't get the girls."

"What do you mean you didn't get the girls? Where the hell are they?"

"I don't know. When we arrived at the dock, the two handlers were dead. And a stranger with a gun fired on us when we approached."

"A stranger with a gun? Why didn't you kill him?"

"We tried, but he was good. Then another showed up. We took heavy fire. Alberto was shot. We had no choice but to leave."

There was a slight pause. Flynn could hear his boss breathing heavily on the other end. Could hear him discussing what to do with people in the room with him.

"Alright, Flynn, here's the deal," his voice came back. Resolute. Like a teacher who'd been pushed over the edge. "I don't care so much about the two blondes. But the third girl, the one with dark hair. Scarlett. She's already sold. We had her up on the black market before we nabbed her." He paused a moment. "It's a hefty fucking sum. And you're going to get her back and bring her here. I don't need to say what will happen to you if you don't, do I?"

He didn't.

"No, boss. But this girl might still have protection. This guy that came—"

"I don't want excuses, Flynn. You find her. You bring her here."

He paused again. Flynn could hear the other voices in the background.

"Duke's apparently in Southern Florida and he can help you," the stern voice added. "You can also have two guys for backup. We'll fly you back to the States as soon as we take care of this little mess you guys just made. Just don't fuck this up, Flynn. You hear me? No mistakes this time."

48

SEVEN

Ange and I moved out into the warm evening air alongside Jack and Lauren. He'd parked my black Tacoma 4x4 right beside Lauren's Sammy. Looking at the Samurai, I didn't know what was more impressive—how the two bad guys had managed to vanish like Houdini, or how all five of them had managed to cram into the tiny off-road vehicle.

"Thanks for taking care of the boat," I said.

The windows were rolled down slightly, and I reached in to pet Atticus through the passenger side.

"No problemo, compadre," he said. "What's the plan for tomorrow?"

I told him that I'd get ahold of the Guard to try and straighten things out. If there were no answers by sunup, I'd take it upon myself to find some.

They climbed into the Sammy and motored off. Ange pulled herself into the passenger side, trying to hold Atty back as he showered her face with licks. As

I moved around the tailgate, I noticed a corner of the tarp in the bed was loose. I'd picked up a quarter-cord of oak firewood earlier that morning from a local friend of ours who'd hauled a trailerful from the mainland. I'd planned to stack them under the house that night to be used in our backyard firepit. But I was too tired. I'd do it in the morning.

Grabbing the loose corner of the blue tarp, I pulled it tight and tucked it under one of the big logs. Once inside, I started up the six-cylinder engine and drove us out of the lot. My house is on Palmetto Street, just a short drive from the hospital. After pulling into the seashell lot, I shut off the engine and climbed out.

The house was painted a light gray color with white trim, and since it was on stilts, it was designed to withstand even the strongest hurricanes and tropical storms. The ground level was used for outdoor storage and for our makeshift gym. The second level had a wraparound porch and views of the yard and channel out back.

We headed upstairs. Atticus smelled something in the driveway, but I coerced him inside with the mention of dinner. After filling his bowl, I headed straight for the master bedroom and crashed on the king-sized bed beside Ange. We were out in seconds, the fatigue of the day taking over.

I woke up naturally at 0400. I've always been an early riser, ever since I can remember. There's something about the quiet of the early-morning hours that I've always enjoyed. It's a time that I can have to myself, to spend working on me and thinking about what I'm going to do that day.

I slid quietly out of bed and headed for the walk-in closet. After pulling on a pair of workout shorts and a cutoff shirt, I laced up my running shoes and downed a glass of water before heading out the door.

The seashell driveway crunched beneath the soles of my shoes as I took off at a slow jog. After about a quarter mile, I felt warmed up. I started the stopwatch on my dive watch, then picked up my speed.

One of my favorite runs in the world is from my house down to the waterfront, then west along the Florida Keys Heritage Trail to Fort Zachary Taylor. From there, the loop up past the Conch Harbor Marina and back to my house is almost exactly eight miles.

I don't like to listen to music when I run. I like to let my senses have their fill. The morning breeze through palm fronds, the soft crashing waves, the soaring gulls, the occasional passing vehicle.

Sometimes motivating myself through the final portions isn't easy. That morning, however, all I had to do was think about the events of the previous evening. I pictured the two guys on the dock. I pictured the three helpless women. And I imagined what would've happened to them if I hadn't been there.

The injustice fueled my resolve to push through the exhaustion. When I reached my mailbox, I clicked the stopwatch and skidded to a stop in my driveway. I bent over with my hands on my knees. My lungs felt like they were about to explode. Air whooshed in and out, and I wiped the sweat from my forehead.

After a few seconds catching my breath, I glanced at the time. Just under forty-eight minutes. A new personal record, and an average mile time of a few seconds under six minutes.

With my run checked off, I strolled toward the house. I stretched as I moved, getting myself limber for the rest of the workout. I had a makeshift gym under my house that consisted of a heavy bag, kettlebells, pull-up bars, and battle ropes. I put myself through one of my hardest circuits and pushed through each punch, pull-up, swing, squat, and minute of planks like they were my last.

When the timer rang out on the final round, I collapsed onto a rubber workout mat. My clothes were drenched in sweat. My heart pounded. I lay there on the mat for a few minutes, then stretched and rose to my feet. Glancing at my watch, I saw that it wasn't even 0530 yet.

Hooyah.

After a shower, I changed into a fresh set of clothes and made a banana, peanut butter, and whey protein shake. Sliding open the glass door, I stepped out onto the second-level porch and looked out over my backyard and channel. The sun was just starting to peek over the distant water and greenery. I took a sip and then quickly downed the rest of it.

I heard footsteps coming from the living room. Looking over my shoulder, I saw Atticus move right up to the glass, his tail wagging against it. Atticus is hit or miss when it comes to early mornings. Sometimes he joins me on my runs, sometimes he grunts and turns his head around for more sleep. He'd been that way this morning, but now it looked like he'd changed his mind.

I finished off the rest of the drink, then noticed that part of my railing was chipping off. Moving closer, I slid my finger over it and thought it might be time to sand it down and relacquer it.

Just as I was about to turn and let my eager dog out, something caught my eye down on the grass. Everything was how we'd left it. The table. The chairs. The firepit.

The hammock was hanging right where it should be, but there was one problem with it: it wasn't empty. There was someone asleep inside it.

A girl.

EIGHT

I recognized her instantly as the young girl from the trio the previous night. She was sound asleep with her head off to the side, facing the channel. Her hair was a mess from the breeze. It covered most of her face.

I watched her for about a minute, perplexed.

Why is she here? And how in the hell did she get here?

My mind ran through possible scenarios like a nineties secretary fingering through a Rolodex. No one at the hospital would have taken her here, especially without telling us. They'd said she'd stay there until she could be picked up. She must've run away. Snuck off in the middle of the night. But how could she have possibly known that this was our house? Key West has a population of around twenty-five thousand. There are hundreds of houses within quick walking distance of the hospital.

Then it hit me.

I left my dirty glass on the outdoor table, strode around the side of the house, and made quick work of the stairs. I headed straight for the back of my Tacoma. Leaning over the bed, I looked over the tarp covering the stacks of firewood. Sure enough, one of the edges was loose again. The same one I'd fixed the previous night.

I lifted it, let go, then directed my gaze toward the backyard.

Smart girl.

If she'd been an enemy of mine, I would've been caught severely off guard. A year in the islands without getting caught up in the action. Maybe I was getting a little too soft in my tropical paradise.

I walked around the house to the backyard. She was still sleeping peacefully, swaying slightly in the soft breeze. She was still dressed the same. Dirty clothes with a few tears.

I stood over her for a few seconds, wondering at her intentions.

"Good morning," I said calmly, but loud enough for her to hear me clearly.

She shifted around and brushed the hair from her face. Our eyes locked for a few seconds, as they had the night before. She looked better. Less scared and well rested.

It was a nice hammock. Ange had bought it on a trip to Curacao a few years back. We'd slept in it before a few nights ourselves, though never without spraying an absurd amount of bug spray and lighting mosquito-repellent candles. She had a few red marks on her face, though not as many as I'd expected.

"Are you going to call the hospital?" she asked, her voice groggy.

"Yes," I replied right away.

She sighed.

"They'll come get me."

"Is that bad?"

"Yes."

"Why?"

She paused a moment. Had to think it over. More like had to decide how much she wanted to tell me. Sitting up in the hammock, she swung her legs over, then buried her face in her hands for a moment before looking up at me.

"I'm not going back," she said.

I shrugged. "It's not my call."

She looked around the yard. "What if I run?"

"Then I'll still call them," I said. "Only difference is you won't get any of my famous mango French toast."

I could almost see her mouth watering behind her lips. Her expression softened.

"I don't want to run. I feel safe here. That's why I came."

"You are safe here. You're safe at the hospital, too."

She was about to say something, but she stopped when she heard the sliding glass door open above us. I glanced up and saw Ange appear, wearing a white tank top and a pair of plaid pajama shorts. She peered down at us and couldn't hide her surprise upon seeing Scarlett.

"Logan, why didn't you tell me we had a guest?" she said from the second-level porch.

I glanced up at her and smiled.

"I wasn't aware myself until a few minutes ago. Scarlett here snuck into the bed of our truck last night."

"I'm impressed," she said. "You must be smart.

And stealthily quiet."

"I am," she stated.

"And humble," I added sarcastically.

"I like a girl who's confident," Ange said with a laugh.

"We were just about to have some French toast," I said.

Ange nodded.

"Sounds delicious. Scarlett, you look like you could use a hot shower."

The young girl lit up and rose to her feet. "Could I ever."

She must've spent half an hour in the bathroom. I guessed that she used just about all of the hot water in our fifty-gallon tank. She turned the knob so far into the red that steam made its way out the bottom of the door and managed to partly fog up our bedroom mirror.

Breakfast had been ready and cooling on the kitchen table for ten minutes by the time she stepped into the living room with a towel wrapped around the top of her head. She was wearing a pair of Ange's denim shorts and a light blue Rubio Charters tee shirt.

She scarfed down three pieces of French toast, two strips of bacon, a pile of scrambled eggs, and two glasses of orange juice. All without a word aside from "thank you."

Having finished eating already, I stepped out onto the deck. Grabbing my phone, I found the number for the hospital and pressed call. After a few rings, I got one of the front desk ladies. I told her what had happened and she was relieved to hear that Scarlett was safe. Apparently, they'd notified the police and had already begun to expect the worst.

After expressing her thanks, she transferred me to

Dr. Patel. Patel was the head physician at the hospital. When he came on the line, he thanked me for taking care of her as well. He was in his early sixties, had a smooth and educated Indian accent, and always got straight to the point.

"If it's alright with you, it might be good for her to stay with people she obviously trusts," he said. "At least until CPS arrives."

"She's an orphan?"

"She's been in and out of various foster homes for most of her life. I got the impression that this kind of behavior is nothing new for her."

I paused a moment. I wasn't surprised. Sex traffickers often target orphans. Some parents are willing to crawl through hell to get their little girls back.

"Any idea when CPS will get here?" I asked.

"They said by tomorrow afternoon. They have to travel down from Orlando. I can give you their contact info."

He did so and I typed it into my phone's note application.

"Alright, we'll watch her, Doc."

"Thank you, Logan. I'll call CPS as well and let them know what happened."

We ended the call and I headed back inside. Scarlett was still going to town on her breakfast, but her pace had slowed a little. I was amazed she had so much space given her thin build.

I sat down and after a few minutes of ravaging like a starving animal, she took a breath.

"You called the hospital?" she said, her eyes boring into mine.

I nodded. She bit her lip and looked down at the table.

"This is really good," she said.

"Really?" Ange said. "I thought you hated it."

She smiled for the first time. Showered and changed into clean clothes, she looked like a completely different girl than the one I'd seen the night before. Her eyes were vibrant, her freckle-spotted face pretty in the early-morning light. At fifteen, she was on the cusp of transitioning from a young girl into a beautiful woman.

Setting her fork down on her barren plate, she finished off the rest of her orange juice. She scanned back and forth between Ange and me.

"Thank you again for the food."

"It's our pleasure, Scarlett," Ange said. "Feel free to eat as much as you like while you're here."

She paused a moment.

"Who are you guys?" she said, asking a question I could tell had been lingering in her mind for a while.

"I told you last night," I said. "I'm Logan and this is my wife, Angelina."

"Not your names. I mean, what do you do for a living?"

Ange and I exchanged glances. Scarlett leaned over the table toward us.

"I was blindfolded last night, but I heard everything," she added. "You went from sounding like a clueless drunk guy to a grade A badass in the blink of an eye. People don't do that kind of thing. Not without a whole lot of training anyway." She glanced over at Ange without skipping a beat. "And you. You took care of us and remained composed the entire time. It was like you'd done it a hundred times. Most people would have freaked out. Most people's pulses would've been well over a hundred beats per minute. I'm guessing yours never went above your resting rate."

The table fell silent. Ange glanced over at me and smiled. She liked this girl. I assumed she reminded her of someone. A younger version of herself, perhaps.

"Let me guess," Ange said. "You're dad's a doctor?"

"One of them was an EMT," she blurted out, then placed a hand over her mouth like she'd said something she hadn't wanted to.

I took in a deep breath and let it out.

"Alright, we'll tell you who we are if you tell us your story," I said. "And why it is that you don't want to go back to the hospital."

NINE

With Atticus restless and with the morning air warming up, we stepped out into the backyard. We sat around the patio, getting to know each other while taking turns tossing the tennis ball out over the lawn.

Scarlett led off. She told us about how she'd been living in various children and foster homes since she was four. She'd lived in seven different locations across Florida during that time. It wasn't the system's fault, she was quick to clear up. She believed they did the best that they could with her. But she had a free spirit, as she explained. She was restless and never felt like she'd found her home.

A few months earlier, she'd started messaging a guy she met online. They chatted for a while, then the guy said that he wanted to meet her. At the time, Scarlett was living at a group home in Miami after running away from her most recent foster home. She said that she snuck out in the middle of the night to meet the guy. Then, after leading her down a dark alley, a bunch of guys grabbed her. They injected her with something that knocked her out then loaded her into a van.

"Do you remember anything about them?" I asked. "The guys who took you."

"I told the investigator yesterday," she said. "The guy wailing on the ground was the one I'd met. He'd said his name was William, but I'm sure that was a lie."

"And do you remember anything from the drive down to the islands?" Ange asked.

Scarlett smiled.

"This is the kind of thing that I'm talking about," she said. "Instead of talking about the weather, or your work schedule, or an upcoming dinner party, you're trying to learn about the guys who took me. Like detectives or something. You're trying to solve this whole thing on your own."

Scarlett looked back and forth between us. Atticus showed up and dropped the saliva-covered tennis ball in the grass in front of her. She picked it up and tossed it across the yard.

"So?" she added. "Now it's both of your turns. You're secret agents or something, I'm guessing?"

"No," I said. "I used to be in the Navy. After I got out, I became a mercenary. That's how I met Ange."

"Mercenaries? Aren't they the bad guys?"

"Sometimes," Ange said. "But we both vetted our jobs carefully. We were guns for hire, yes. But we never accepted a job if the ethics were in question."

"So, you kill bad guys for a living?"

"Killed," I said. "I told you we don't do it anymore. But essentially, yeah. Every job's a little different. Some were more intel gathering. Some asset protection. But yes, killing bad guys was usually involved."

She fell quiet for a moment, mulling something over. Ange and I both waited for her to spit it out.

"Is it hard?" she said. "Killing people, that is. Like that guy last night. How do you feel afterward?"

I was taken slightly off guard. It was a good question. An important question. One that I'd never expect from someone so young.

I paused a moment but didn't have to think long. I'd pondered such things for years. I never had a hard time dealing with it so long as the proper justification existed.

"Those guys who took you," I finally said. "You're not the first. Odds are they've taken hundreds of women. Innocent young girls on their way to school. Out with friends. Walking down a dark street." I paused a moment, then continued, "Taken from everything they know. Drugged. Beaten. Forced to do things you can't imagine. Then killed and tossed aside like smelly garbage. Do you think those guys deserved what I did to them?"

She swallowed hard. Nodded.

"Yes," she said. "You're right. They did deserve it. So you don't lose sleep over it?"

"No," I said.

She glanced at Ange.

"Never," she said. "You sure you're fifteen?" she added with a smile.

Scarlett grinned at the compliment. Atticus showed up for what seemed like the hundredth round. If he was tired, he sure didn't show it. Scarlett was a good sport. She grabbed the slobber-covered ball and tossed it again.

Turning back to us, she said, "So you've both

fought a lot of bad guys before, then?"

I nodded.

"That's a pretty unique job. What do you do now? For work, I mean."

Ange and I exchanged glances. I gave her the floor.

"We don't," Ange said. "We're retired."

"You're too young to retire."

"You can retire at any age," I said with a smile. "Though it's more semi-retired. We get swooped up into adventures from time to time."

We told her about a few of them—just summaries, really. The big pictures of various dangerous and exciting escapades we'd gotten ourselves into since we'd moved to the island chain. No gory details. Purely PG-13 versions.

She was intrigued, hanging on every word, and wanted to know more.

After half an hour of storytime, Atticus finally showed signs of fatigue. He ran with feigned enthusiasm, tennis ball lodged in his mouth, then plopped down in the grass beside Scarlett.

"You wore him out," I said, rising to my feet and stretching. "It's a miracle." I glanced up toward the house and added, "Heading for a drink run. Either of you want anything?"

I took the girls' orders, strode up to the kitchen, then returned with three glasses. Two lemonades and a glass of ice water. I handed the lemonades to the girls and looked out over the channel.

"What was that move you did on the dock?" Scarlett said after chugging down the entire glass. "The one you used to take down the first guy."

"Just a standard hip throw," I said. "With a broken arm added for kicks."

"Judo, right?"

I looked at Ange, whose eyebrows were raised.

"You know martial arts?" I asked.

"Was one of your foster dads Mr. Miyagi?" Ange added.

Scarlett chuckled. She was so young that I was surprised she got the reference.

"Sort of. He was a taekwondo instructor. I lived in their house for almost two years and spent a lot of time at his dojang. Can you show me the move you did last night?"

I smiled and nodded. We migrated out onto the open grass and faced off. Ange leaned back, adjusted her sunglasses, then took a sip of lemonade.

"Alright," I said. "I'll be me at first, and you'll be thug number one. Now, come at me slowly with a right hook."

She did so. I lunged toward her, grabbed her softly by the arm, rotated, and pressed my hips against her body as I dropped down. I was gentle and slow, and I talked through my moves. We repeated the action, reversing our roles. She was a quick learner.

"So what if it's reversed?" she said. "What if one of those big guys had me from behind? What should I do?"

"No sweat. Even with the size difference, you'd just need to make a few tweaks to your technique." I demonstrated the move.

Ange smiled and clapped when Scarlett replicated it. Using her body properly as leverage, she was able to lift me off the ground. In the heat of the moment, with her adrenaline pumping, I had no doubt she'd be able to perform the move successfully even on a bigger guy than me.

"Another great option is to just break their

fingers," Ange said. "The bones are fragile, so it's easily done. It's an underrated yet incredibly effective move."

She was really excited to learn new defense moves. It was clear that she'd used her time with her instructor foster father well.

"Could you teach me to fight like you do?" she said after half an hour of sparring. "With guns and other weapons, I mean."

I laughed. "Sure. But why would you need to?"

"Maybe I can do what you both did. I could travel and fight bad guys someday."

Ange walked over and tossed us each a towel. "It's a hard life," she said. "Not for the faint of heart. Nor is it a decision to be made lightly."

We wiped the sweat from our faces.

"How did you get into it?" Scarlett asked Ange. "You don't look like a mercenary."

"That's why she was so good," I said. "Among other reasons, of course."

She patted Scarlett on the shoulder. "Mine's a long story. Maybe someday I'll tell you more, but for now, I was an orphan and had a strong disliking for evil men."

"An orphan?" Scarlett said with a faint smile. "Like me."

My phone vibrated in my pocket, ruining the touching moment. I grabbed it and saw that I was getting a call from a good friend of mine, Scott Cooper.

"Excuse me," I said and stepped over toward the house and up the stairs.

I entered through the side door, then plopped down on the living room sofa, where I had a three-way call with Scott Cooper and CIA Deputy Director Wilson.

66

Scott and I went way back. We'd served together in the Navy, where we became good friends, and we've kept in close touch over the years. Smart and a natural leader, Scott was currently serving as a senator representing Florida.

"The Coast Guard did a thorough search of that freighter and came up empty," Wilson said, getting straight to the guts of it. He had a rich Georgia accent. "They also did background checks on the crew. They were all clean as can be. It's possible that we could be wrong, but it appears as though the freighter wasn't involved."

"It had to have been involved," I said. "I was there. I watched the scene unfold. The boat was less than two hundred yards ahead of us when the freighter came in. By the time it passed, it was gone."

"I said it appears as though it wasn't involved," Wilson added. "But that doesn't mean we're ruling it out. Freighters smuggling illegal items is nothing new. Which is why we're tracking it and all shipping activity more carefully."

"There's no reason why a freighter should have been that close to the Lower Keys, right?" Scott said.

"They shouldn't have been that close, no," Wilson said. "They were about eighty miles east of the normal shipping lane from Tampa to Havana."

"How did they explain that?" I asked.

Wilson didn't skip a beat. "The captain said their navigation equipment was malfunctioning," he said. "Apparently, they just managed to correct it in time before running aground."

We fell silent. None of us were buying that. The freighter had been off course, cruising at full speed, and the boat had disappeared behind it—one too many coincidences.

"I'll contact you both once I have anything more," Wilson said. "For now, good work bringing those guys down. We have the guy whose leg you shattered in custody and we're hopeful we can get him to talk."

We ended the call. I stood still for a moment, lost in thought, then stepped back out into the yard.

With Scott and Wilson on top of it, I was confident that it wouldn't take long for one of them to dig up a lead.

TEN

After another hour of relaxing, intermittent sparring, and sharing a few pearls of wisdom, we decided to take the boat out for an afternoon on the water. With Scott, the CIA, and the Coast Guard tackling the missing boat mystery, there wasn't much I could do to help. At least for the time being.

Ange had suggested that going out on the boat might not be a good idea. She assumed, for good reason, that Scarlett would need her rest after all she'd been through.

"I'm not tired," she said enthusiastically.

"Are you sure?" I asked.

"It sounds fun."

We loaded everything up, then locked the house.

"Ever been diving?" Ange asked Scarlett as she helped us carry a cooler and a few bags across the backyard.

"Like diving into a pool?"

Ange and I both laughed.

"I'll take that as a no," Ange said. "Looks like today's gonna be your first lesson."

There's a small boathouse on the edge of the channel where I kept our 22 Robalo center-console. Once we had everything loaded, I lowered the boat into the water using two davits. We moved down the concrete steps and climbed aboard. Inserting the key, I started up the 200-hp engine and began the beautiful commute to the marina.

"Where's the diving stuff?" Scarlett said, looking around the boat.

"It's all on the boat," I replied.

She looked around again, then looked at me like I was crazy.

"The other boat," Ange said, hitting me playfully. "We prefer to take the skiff over the truck when the weather's nice."

"Less traffic," I said with a grin.

Fifteen minutes later, I brought us into the Conch Harbor Marina, and we tied off beside the Baia. The marina is a short walk from downtown and just north of the famous Mallory Square. With two long docks, each with eight fingers on each side, the marina usually has well over forty boats of various shapes and sizes tied off. The *Yankee Freedom* ferry to Dry Tortugas National Park sets sail just up the waterfront, and the Key West Coast Guard sector is just beyond it.

I've had the Baia moored here since the day I bought it. Slip twenty-four, just a few slips down from where Jack keeps his boat moored at slip forty-seven. I peeked over and couldn't see the Conch Republic and Jolly Roger flags marking the top of his boat, the *Calypso*. He was already out on the water.

Day two of lobster season. Christmas morning round two.

Scarlett stared at the Baia in awe for a few seconds as I climbed over and dropped a bag in the cockpit.

"This is your boat?" she asked. Before receiving a reply, she added, "How rich are you guys?"

Easy on the eyes, Baia Flashes have the perfect combination of speed, style, and comfort. The Italian-made thing of beauty turns more heads than a Ferrari.

When I'd moved back to the Keys in the spring of '08, I'd taken one quick glance at the housing costs before deciding that a live-aboard life was the life for me. I used savings I'd accumulated over the years, as well as some of the money my dad had left me after his death, to buy it. The house had come later. Finding the Aztec treasure and accepting a finder's fee had bankrolled that purchase.

"What? You're not going to rob us, are you?" I asked.

It was a genuine possibility. I'd seen this story play out before in movies and books. People lend a helping hand to someone down on their luck, only to be taken advantage of. A very common tale. The fact that she was a runaway orphan didn't help her case. But there was something about her. Ange and I had both seen it already. We liked her.

Still, I kept a sharp eye on her.

"I wouldn't know where to start," she said with a laugh. "No, I saw what you did to those guys on the dock, remember? Plus, you did save my life."

We transferred our stuff over to the Baia.

It was just after 1100 by the time we cast off. Already well over eighty degrees, it was also less cloudy than the previous day. Bright blue sky shone crisp from horizon to horizon. There were a few small patches of clouds here and there. A seven-knot breeze blew in from the east, carrying with it the smells of saltwater, nearby restaurant aromas, and faint boat fuel fumes.

I brought us slowly out of the harbor. Scarlett and Atticus were up on the bow. I'm not sure who was more excited. They looked all around them, taking in every sight and sound. I've been on a boat with many different types of people. Few don't like it, some are indifferent. Most take in the primal feeling of being out on the water with genuine happiness. Every now and then, however, you witness someone experiencing nothing short of pure ecstatic bliss. It was like she'd been a fish flapping on land her whole life and had just been tossed into water for the first time.

"Alright, come on down," I said as I brought us out of the opening into the harbor.

I was about to bring us up to speed. With no bow railing, the last thing I wanted was for her to tumble over the side as I brought us up on plane.

She nodded and climbed around the windscreen with Atticus right behind her. Her face was big and bright, her eyes full of life. I couldn't believe that this was the same girl I'd seen the previous night.

"This is so beautiful," she said, her smile so big it looked like her face might rip apart.

"Yes, it is," Ange said.

She wrapped an arm around Scarlett's waist and motioned for her to sit down.

"Hold on," I said.

I slid the throttles all the way forward, throwing us back as the bow rose up high in the water. Scarlett loved it. Soon I had us up to our cruising speed, motoring south along the edge of Key West and into the straits.

Ten minutes later, we dropped anchor at our destination seven miles southeast of Key West. There were a few other boats anchored in view, the closest being a small bowrider a few hundred yards off that I didn't recognize. We were over sixty feet of water, and I didn't need to look over the side to tell the visibility. It's almost always over seventy feet in most parts of the Keys, especially that far offshore.

Scarlett stepped out from the saloon behind Ange. They'd both changed into swimsuits, Ange into a teal bikini and Scarlett into a dark blue one-piece. Fortunately, she and Ange were nearly the same size. Scarlett looked excited and eager to get in the water.

"First order of business is a swim test," I said.

She splashed in off the swim platform and did a quick lap around the boat. She was good, relaxed, in good shape, and she knew the strokes well. I handed her a mask and snorkel, and she peered down at the underwater world.

"It's amazing," she said, popping her head up after half a minute of staring. "There's so much going on down there. So much life."

We learned on the ride over that she'd never lived, or even visited, south of Miami before. And she'd never been so much as snorkeling in the ocean before. For her, tropical fish existed only in pet stores and in fancy lobbies in movies.

Ange and I took a dip as well. After five minutes, we climbed out, toweled off, and went over the basics of scuba diving. We grabbed her a BCD and taught her each of the components and what they do. Then she slid into a wetsuit and strapped it over her back with a tank of air. You can explain what it's like until your throat hurts, but nothing beats getting in the water and feeling it for yourself.

We helped her down to the swim platform, then handed her a pair of fins. Once on, she spat into her mask and swirled the saliva around the inside of the lenses. After rinsing it off in the water, she strapped the mask over her eyes.

"How do I look?" she said, turning to us and striking a pose.

I laughed.

"Like a scuba supermodel," Ange said. She handed me her phone, then climbed down and posed alongside her. "In fact, I think a picture is necessary to commemorate this moment," she added.

I brought up the camera and lined it up. They both struck a pose, and I counted down, then snapped a shot. Then Ange wanted another with Scarlett's mask down. I took it, then stepped over and handed the phone to them. They both hovered over the screen and inspected it, Ange shielding the sun from their faces.

"Looks like it belongs in a magazine," Ange said.

Once in the water, we properly weighted Scarlett to counteract the positive buoyancy of her body, wetsuit, and gear. Then it was time for her to drop down—only a few feet at first, just to get a feel for it. Breathing in and out of the regulator was strange at first. She breathed quickly but soon slowed and calmed herself. She used the power inflator button to control her depth well by venting and filling air into the BCD's air bladder. I smiled as I watched her through my mask while treading water. She was a natural.

I taught her a few quick necessary skills. First, how to clear her mask when water filled inside. A simple tilt back of the head and a forceful exhale through the nose. Then I taught her how to find her regulator if it ever fell from her mouth. It wasn't the official PADI open water certification course by any means, but it was enough for her to understand how it worked. Besides, we'd be right by her side in case anything went wrong.

Once ready, she climbed up and sat on the swim platform. Ange and I donned our gear. Scarlett was going off about how cool it was to breathe underwater. Even though I was seven when I went on my first dive, I can still remember it clearly. It was in the Red Sea with my dad, and it was one of the most exciting experiences of my life.

Once ready to go, we stepped down and Ange sat beside Scarlett to don her fins.

Before dropping in, I filled Atticus's water bowl, then gave him a handful of treats. I cracked open a few of the windows to give him a nice breeze.

"You're in charge, boy," I said, then shut the saloon door and headed for the stern.

The three of us splashed into the water and descended. A world of colorful marine life opened its doors and surrounded us. We reached the bottom and finned along the reef. Up ahead, I spotted our destination—Joe's Tug, one of the most popular dive sites in the Lower Keys. Despite its name, it's actually a seventy-five-foot shrimp boat that originally sank back in '86 before being raised and eventually resunk for the artificial reef program.

The wreck was broken in two pieces, with about thirty feet separating the forward and aft sections. We approached from the bow, the barnacle-encrusted hull appearing through the water like a ghost ship. Scarlett's reaction was just as I'd hoped. Here she was diving for her first time, and she was diving a tropical reef and wreck. Sure beat a swimming pool.

The current was calm, and the bright sun far overhead made everything vibrant. Taking in the sights, we finned around the wreck, Ange and I keeping a sharp eye on Scarlett. She was very comfortable in the water for her first dive.

We spotted a few moray eels as well as barracuda. We were also happy to find the wreck's most famous inhabitant was in the building. Elvis looked even bigger than the last time I'd seen him. A massive goliath grouper estimated to weigh over seven hundred pounds. There were two other groups of divers, not surprising given the time of day and popularity of the wreck.

I finned over the deck of the wreck, enjoying the dive thoroughly. Glancing at my dive watch, I saw that we'd been down half an hour. Using hand signals, I asked Scarlett how much air she had left. She informed me that she still had twelve hundred pounds left in her tank. Ange and I both still had fifteen hundred, so I figured we could spend at least another ten or even twenty minutes at depth if we wanted.

Suddenly, the sound of a distant engine caught my attention. I glanced up, looking for the source of the sound.

It was getting louder.

I scanned back and forth and soon spotted a boat. It was motoring toward the Baia from the north, and it was going pretty fast given all the dive flags in the water.

I reached for the carabiner strapped to my BCD. Three quick taps against my tank got the girls' attention. I motioned up toward the approaching boat, then motioned for them to stay there.

I thought about the guys who'd gotten away the previous night. Who'd motored out into the Gulf and vanished.

It wasn't the same boat we'd chased off into the night. I could tell that much even from sixty feet down. But maybe they'd switched boats. Maybe they'd stolen a new one and tracked me down somehow to try and exact their revenge. I told myself it was almost impossible, but I'd witnessed enough nearly impossible things in my life to always prepare for the worst.

Looking up, I finned for the surface.

ELEVEN

I kept my eyes glued on the boat's hull, watching its every movement as I ascended. I moved with a purpose. Fifty, thirty-five, twenty feet. There was no time for the recommended three-minute safety stop at fifteen feet down.

I watched as the boat pulled up alongside the starboard side of the Baia. Shifting my course, I kicked for the port side.

At five feet down, I took in a short breath, then reached behind me and twisted my tank's valve shut. Then I pressed the purge button on my regulator to vent out the remaining air. The last thing I wanted was for my regulator to accidentally face upward after surfacing. The release of pressurized air would be loud enough to give away my position.

Holding the shallow breath, I finned for the surface. I broke through with my body up against the port gunwale. Quickly undoing the straps and Velcro,

I slid out of my BCD and fins and reached for my dive knife. While diving, I kept it strapped to the inside of my right calf.

I planned out my moves. A quick look, a quick fling of my knife if necessary, and a dive for my Sig that was lodged in a narrow locker under the helm.

Reaching overhead, I pressed my fingers to the top of the gunwale and pulled myself up out of the water. I heard voices coming from the idling boat. The second I peeked over the side with my knife drawn back, I gasped and relaxed down onto my side.

"Holy shit," Cal Brooks said. He was standing at the stern of his white Privateer Pilothouse, *Zig-Zag*, with his hands raised above his head. "We come in peace, Logan."

I pulled myself up the rest of the way and sat on the sunbed while I slid my knife back into its sheath. Just a false alarm. I won't have to wipe any blood from the blade. At least not today.

Cal owned Conch Republic Divers, a small operation out of Boot Key. There was a large group at his back. They were sitting and facing each other while going over their gear for an upcoming dive, but a few of them had noticed my brief inhospitable behavior.

"Why so jumpy?" Cal said, lowering his sunglasses.

"Sorry, Cal," I said.

I reached over the gunwale, grabbed my floating BCD and fins, then hauled them up into my boat. Then I slid off the sunbed and walked over to the port gunwale.

"I had a bit of a long night."

"Permission to come aboard?"

I told him to go ahead, and he climbed over. A

member of his crew had thrown over a couple of fenders to keep our hulls from scratching each other.

"I heard about that," he said. "Any word on the ones that got away?"

I shook my head.

"Not yet." I glanced over at the antsy group on his boat. "What can I do for you?"

"The heel of one of our fins split," he said. "I know you wear men's large, so I was checking to see if you had an extra pair."

"I thought you had every piece of dive equipment in existence on that boat."

"Everything except what I need," he said with a laugh. "Like looking for the right-sized lid in a Tupperware drawer."

I spotted a few bubbles break the surface beside the stern. I shook my head, then grabbed the carabiner from my BCD and stepped down to the swim platform. I crouched at the edge and dipped my right hand underwater. I tapped the hull with the carabiner, then gave the OK signal so Ange would know that everything was alright.

Rising to my feet, I grabbed my extra fins from the storage space under the sunbed and handed them to Cal. He thanked me.

"Maybe I'll see you at Pete's later," he said as he untied the line. "It's karaoke night."

"Not sure you could pay me enough to hear you sing the Cranberries again."

He laughed. I'd had "Zombie" stuck in my head for two days after the last karaoke night. And not the good version.

"Might have to change it up tonight."

He thanked me again. They motored slowly to the other side of the wreck site and anchored closer to the other boats. It was like an armada of charters now.

Ange and Scarlett surfaced after performing the recommended safety stop. They both removed their gear in the water, and I hauled it up and set it down with mine beside the transom.

"False alarm?" Ange said as she climbed up the ladder behind Scarlett.

"Just Cal," I said, pointing over at his boat. "He needed some fins."

"I thought he had everything on that boat."

The three of us slid out of our wetsuits and toweled off. I let Atticus out and tossed his tennis ball a few times so that he could enjoy the water as well. Scarlett and Ange brought up a few lobster rolls and coconut waters from the galley. We sat and scarfed down while taking in the sights. Scarlett was unusually quiet. She'd expressed that she enjoyed the dive, but she clearly had something on her mind.

"Who did you think that was?" she said after being pressed.

"I wasn't sure." I chewed and swallowed another bite.

"You thought it could be the guys that you chased last night?"

"I thought there was a chance. I don't like being taken off guard."

She took a few bites and thought for a moment. "I don't think they'll come back," she said confidently. "I think you taught them a lesson."

"I hope you're right," I said.

If only lessons could be learned that easily. But I'd dealt with those types of people for most of my life. I could have scared them off, or I could have just pissed them off.

"Cal also wanted to make sure we were alright," I

told Ange. "He's keeping a look out for anything suspicious."

Ange nodded.

"How does he already know what happened?" Scarlett asked. "Is he a close friend of yours?"

"It's called the Coconut Telegraph," Ange said. "Conchs tell their friends, then they tell their friends. Pretty soon it's common knowledge on every island. Never underestimate the Coconut Telegraph."

Paying homage to the king, I played my Elvis's Greatest Hits playlist on the outdoor speakers. We finished eating to "Jailhouse Rock," relaxed for an hour, then cruised west to Neptune's Table for a shallower dive.

We spent the rest of the day out on the water. We taught Scarlett more about diving and how to read currents, charts, and weather patterns. We also taught her basic boat operation and terminology. She was a quick learner. By the time the sun was setting, she was at the helm, bringing us back into Conch Harbor.

After tying off, we rinsed down all of our gear, then tidied up. Once everything was stowed, I locked up the Baia and we all climbed aboard the Robalo and motored back to the house.

Even when living in the tropics, there's nothing better after a day of diving than a long hot shower. Once clean and dressed in fresh clothes, we sat out on the porch and talked enthusiastically about the day.

"You two have an incredible life," Scarlett said while petting Atticus and looking out over the water.

It hadn't come easy or without risks. But she was right. The life Ange and I shared was better than anything I could've possibly imagined.

Ange glanced at her watch. It was 1930. The mic was scheduled to get hot at Pete's in half an hour.

"Who's hungry?" Ange said.

We climbed into the Tacoma and drove downtown. Salty Pete's Bar, Grill, and Museum is one of my favorite places on earth. It's located just a few blocks from the busy streets of Duval and Whitehead and has been a landmark in Key West ever since the owner, Pete Jameson, opened the doors over thirty years ago.

I pulled us into the nearly full seashell parking lot. By outward appearance, Pete's place looks more like an old renovated house than a restaurant. A two-story wooden structure with a balcony out back and a modest porch and front door.

We entered, welcomed by the ring of a bell and the chorus of various conversations. The main dining area was nearing max capacity and the staff was busy shuffling meals and taking orders. Assorted pictures and maritime memorabilia covered the walls. It was well renovated but still had its classic feel.

Mia, the lead waitress, welcomed us and said that Pete was up getting things ready on the balcony. We headed up the wooden staircase at the back of the room. The second level is the museum part, filled with rows of various artifacts from around the Keys, most kept in glass cases.

Ange and I headed for the sliding glass door to the balcony, but we quickly realized that Scarlett had veered off course. She was drawn to the displays like a mosquito to a zapper light. She was particularly interested in the artifacts we'd managed to keep from the Aztec treasure. And the chest we'd found buried last year over at the base of the Key West Lighthouse.

"The sides of the chest are riddles," I said. "We had to meet up with a scholarly friend of ours to figure out how to open it."

"Who made it?" she asked. "And why?"

There were a few placards with brief explanations of the adventure, but I told her that we'd give her the full story sometime.

"Who's that scary-looking guy?" she asked, pointing at the large image of a pirate as we headed toward the door.

"A pirate captain named John Shadow," Ange said. "And that's a whole other story."

She moved slowly, enjoying all the displays. "You think I could ever help you find something like this?" she asked, motioning toward a picture of the excavation of Shadow's treasure trove on Lignumvitae Key.

"Sure," I said. "You keep progressing like you did today and you'll be an aquanaut in no time."

The glass door slid open, allowing the loud outside commotion to take the place of the relative quiet. We looked up and spotted Pete. We left the door open for one of the waitresses, then smiled as he moved toward us.

Pete is one of the most well-liked people in the islands. He's as conch as can be, having lived his whole life in the Keys and spent much of it on the water. He's in his early sixties, with tanned skin from hours spent out under the sun. He's average height and has a noticeable beer gut and a bald head. But he has a spring and liveliness to his movements that's uncommon for his age. The most distinguishing characteristic, however, is the shiny hook he has instead of a right hand.

"Well, if it isn't the Dodges," he said with a big smile. "I feel like I haven't seen you in ages."

"We saw you a few days ago," Ange said with a laugh.

Much like Jack, Pete lived on island time.

"Who's this?" he said.

"Scarlett," I said, then introduced them. "She's staying with us until tomorrow."

"Pleasure to meet you," he said, giving her a hug. "Any friend of Logan and Ange is a friend of mine. I heard about what happened. It was a good thing you stumbled upon them, Logan."

The Coconut Telegraph strikes again.

He led us to an empty table off to the side. The karaoke was just about to start up when Mia came over with a stack of menus.

"What's your favorite thing here?" Scarlett asked while looking over the menu.

"That's like asking what's the best Tom Hanks movie," I said. "There are too many great ones to decide. What do you like?"

We ordered the works and shared buffet style. A blackened grouper sandwich. Shrimp cocktail. Conch fritters. A dozen raw oysters on the half shell. A plate of their famous sweet potato fries. In essence, pure bliss. Scarlett approved, loving everything she tasted.

Jack and Lauren joined the group just as the music started.

As is the case at most every karaoke night around the world, the singing started off pretty good. Then, as the drinks tallied up and the confidence levels rose, things got ugly. It's like watching *American Idol*. There are the good ones, and then there are the ones who should never attempt a note outside of their shower under normal circumstances. But that's what makes karaoke so fun. There's no pressure, and it's all just about having a good time.

As we finished eating, Cal Brooks stumbled up to the stage. He hadn't lied earlier about changing it up.

Instead of his usual song choice, he decided on a personal rendition of "My Heart Will Go On" by Celine Dion. I haven't laughed so hard in a long time, and by the end of it, half the people were on their feet and holding their arms out like Rose on *Titanic*'s bow.

He finished to roaring applause. I took my last bite of food and stared in awe as Scarlett downed the rest of her second plate.

"I don't know where you put it all," I said.

It really was incredible, considering I estimated that she couldn't weigh more than a buck ten.

"You were right," she said. "It's all just so good."

A few songs later, she asked where the bathroom was, and Ange and Lauren stood up to go with her. As the three of them headed toward the door, I spotted a guy I'd never seen before. He looked young, probably early twenties, with sunburned skin and a skinny frame. He was wearing big goofy sunglasses, even though the sun had been down for a few hours. He also wore a strange silver chain, a mostly unbuttoned Hawaiian shirt, jeans, and sandals. He stood out, which isn't easy to do in the ultra-liberal Key West.

His look didn't bother me. What bothered me was that he was staring at the three girls when they passed by him. Not a friendly or even just a quick checking-them-out look either. His mouth opened, and he lowered his sunglasses for a better look.

I was used to guys checking out Ange. When you have a wife as beautiful as she is, it comes with the territory. But this guy made no attempt at being discreet, or respectful.

I watched him after they walked past. Sure enough, he stared at them until they disappeared from view. Then he grabbed his phone. He had all the makings of a real pervert. If he aimed the camera of his phone anywhere near them when they came back, I'd have no choice but to walk over and introduce myself.

"You alright, bro?" Jack said.

I looked away from the mysterious guy and faced Jack and Pete.

"You recognize that guy?" I asked, motioning toward the stranger.

They both looked then shook their heads.

Suddenly, my phone vibrated to life in my pocket. I slid it out and saw a new message. It was from Scott. He told me that they had a lead. A crewmember from the freighter last night wanted to meet with me. He claimed to have seen what had happened to the lost boat. He was back at his home in Tampa, and Scott wanted to fly me out there in the morning. Why he couldn't just tell everything on the phone, I didn't know, but I figured he wanted to keep things confidential. Maybe he didn't want to lose his job.

I texted back, saying I was able to go. Then I got another message a minute later saying Scott would have his helicopter pick me up at Key West International the following morning. It sounded like a good lead. Maybe it could help us put a stop to the entire operation.

After replying, I lowered my phone.

Just as I lifted my eyes from the screen of my phone, I saw the girls walking back toward us. They weaved through a few standing people. Scarlett, who was taking up the rear, waited as a busboy moved past with a gray tub of dirty dishes. The guy I'd noticed before was sitting just a table away from her. He was staring at her intently, eyeing her up and down. It was a look I'd seen many times before. A harmless, natural look most of the time. Just not when it's a grown man checking out a fifteen-year-old girl.

As Scarlett headed our way and closer to the guy, I slid my chair back a foot. I was ready to rise from my seat and pounce. I could be over there in a few seconds.

The guy released his grip on his beer and moved his arm back. He didn't take her picture. As Scarlet strode by his table, he shifted his body, leaned forward, and slapped her butt with his right hand.

TWELVE

I was up from my seat in an instant. Before the young punk's hand struck. My legs lifted me and moved the rest of my body toward the incident uncontrollably.

I couldn't hear anything over the singing, but I'd seen it. As clear as day. I'd seen it, and it was time to teach the guy a lesson.

But I was beaten to it.

Mere seconds after the guy made contact, Scarlett spun around and snatched his wrist with her right hand. Faster than a blink, she jerked him down, pressed her left hand onto the top of his neck, and slammed his head into the corner of his table. The glasses and plates shook as his skull hit the pointed edge with a thud. He yelled, then toppled over. Not unconscious, but dazed from the blow.

Unrelenting, Scarlett jammed her right foot onto his chest, pinning him to the deck. Ange reached her first, with me right on her heels.

89

"What the fuck was that for?" the guy shouted as best he could in between groans of pain.

There was a gash in his forehead. Blood dripped down the side of his face. The guy singing had seen the commotion and stopped, leaving only the background instrumental as all eyes gravitated toward the scene.

"Touch me again and it'll only get worse," Scarlett snapped.

The guy tried to force her foot off, but she only pressed harder. I wanted to close in and give the guy a piece of my mind, but Ange stopped me.

"Shit, I was just showing some affection," the guy barked. "You should be flattered."

Now I'd had enough.

"She's fifteen, jackass," I said, sliding a table to move beside Scarlett. "You show her affection again and you'll be spending the next month in a hospital bed."

He eyed me with intense rage. One of the lenses of his big goofy sunglasses had shattered. Somehow they'd managed to stay on his face. He looked like an idiot, and he'd just gotten his butt handed to him by a teenaged girl.

"Hey," he said, finally able to come up with a reply. "Who the hell do you—"

Scarlett shifted her foot down over his neck to shut him up.

"It's time for you to leave," she said.

His face went from angry as hell to stoic in a second. He nodded slowly.

"I'm very sorry," he said calmly. "I'll leave."

His tone shifted as well, from angry to more pleasant. As pleasant as I pegged him capable of anyway. It was like the guy suffered from multiple personality disorder or something.

Scarlett kept the pressure on him for a few seconds, then let off. He staggered to his feet and wiped the blood from his face with a napkin. I watched him like a hawk. If he made so much as a move toward her, I'd have him laid out and begging for mercy.

"You have a pleasant evening," he said, bowing to her.

There was something very off about his behavior. Something deeply sinister. The entire crowd was watching by that point. By all outward appearances, he'd gotten spooked and decided it best to shape up and leave. But I sensed a desire for revenge and expected him to snap at any second.

He didn't.

He set the napkin on the table, turned around, and walked casually away. He moved through the sliding glass door and soon disappeared from view.

A few people in the crowd began to clap. Then more joined in. Within seconds there were loud cheers thrown into the mix.

Pete patted Scarlett on the back.

"An impressive display," he said. Then he turned to look at Ange and me and added, "You sure she's not related to you?"

"A good move," Ange said. "Nicely done."

I couldn't stop staring at the glass door, couldn't get the punk out of my mind.

Something about him wasn't right. I'd seen a lot of bar fights in my time. Never had I seen someone get hit, then brush themselves off and walk away cordially.

Maybe he was a nutjob. He certainly looked the part.

As the music started back up, I walked over to Mia.

"I'm surprised you didn't teach that guy a lesson," she said when she locked eyes on me.

She unfolded a wooden tray stand, then set a platter of food on top of it.

"She beat me to it," I replied with a smile. "Hey, I noticed that punk was drinking. You didn't happen to card him, did you?"

She set a few full plates in front of happy patrons.

"His last name was Duke," she said, already knowing what my next question was going to be. "That's all I remember."

I thanked her, gave her a hand with the remaining plates, then moved back to my table.

After the excitement wore off, we spent another hour listening to the songs and enjoying some drinks and Key lime pie. I couldn't get over how well Scarlett had handled herself. That guy had been much bigger and stronger than her, and yet she'd managed to take him down. She was even more like Ange than I thought.

THIRTEEN

We drove home at half past ten. It had been another long day and we were all looking forward to a good night's sleep.

"You did good today," I told Scarlett as we stepped into the living room. "And not just with the drunk guy. I mean with everything. You've got a bright future ahead of you. I can feel it."

She stared at me for a few seconds. Frozen solid. Then she took two steps, wrapped her arms around me, and pressed herself into my chest. I smiled as I hugged her back. She sniffled a few times. I glanced over at Ange, who was getting teary-eyed as well.

Without a word, she released her grip. Stepping back, she wiped her face with her hand, then turned and moved toward the spare bedroom. She petted a sleepy Atticus, then stopped when she reached the doorway and looked back over her shoulder.

"I wish I didn't have to leave," she said.

Then she entered and shut the door behind her.

Ange and I stood quiet for a moment. When I tilted my head and our eyes met, she had a faint smile on her face. A knowing smile.

"What?" I said.

"Nothing," she lied.

We crawled into bed and switched off the lights. Atticus nestled into his bed on the floor. Our curtains were shut but rippled slightly from the breeze entering the partly open window. A few cracks of distant glowing moonlight snuck through and allowed me to see a few dark swaying palms.

I lay on my back and wrapped my arm around Ange. Instead of snuggling up with her head on my chest, she sat up.

"What if," she said, finally letting out all the thoughts I knew were bouncing around in her mind, "she didn't have to leave?"

Now it was my turn to sit up.

"What do you mean?"

"Well, I mean what if we adopt her?"

I flipped on my bedside lamp. I wanted to look her in the eyes.

Had she had a little too much to drink? Was she joking or something?

The light flicked on. She was looking right at me. Serious.

"Ange, we—"

"I called her case manager," she cut me off. "While on the boat. I used the sat phone. I was just curious how the process works."

It was something I'd honestly never even thought about. Maybe because it was so sudden and so far out of left field.

Left field? More like the parking garage two

94

blocks from the stadium.

"Ange, I like her too, but we barely know her. And you want to become legally responsible for her?"

"Look, I know it's more than a little crazy. But she doesn't have anyone." She paused a moment, biting her lip. "I just think we can help her. In a few years she'll be an adult. I think maybe we can help steer her in the right direction."

I fell silent, lost in thought. Ange wasn't just describing Scarlett, she was describing herself. Having lost both her parents at a young age, Ange had been left to the foster system as well. A different country. A different time. But still similar. She knew as well as anyone how much of an influence we could have, even in just a few years' time.

I took in a deep breath and let it out.

"What did she say?" I finally asked. When she tilted her head, I added, "Scarlett's case manager."

She smiled, then told me about the conversation they'd had. Adoption wouldn't be a difficult process given the circumstances. To begin the process, we of course needed to start by filling out an application and submitting to background checks. From there, the case manager said it could take anywhere from eight months to well over a year. In the meantime, Scarlett would still be picked up the following day and taken back to their group home in Miami.

"I'll think about it, Ange. It's not something to be decided lightly."

"I agree," she said, shifting down and resting her head on my chest. "We'll think it over. But I hope it works out. I really do think we can help her, Logan."

I switched off the light, then slid down to get more comfortable. I agreed with her, thought we could help her. But the fact remained that we'd just met her. We barely knew her, and we'd need to spend time rectifying that before I'd agree to something so major as adopting her.

"What do you want to do tomorrow?" Ange asked after a few seconds of silence.

"I forgot to tell you. I'm meeting with Scott. He messaged me earlier and said they've got a possible lead."

"The sex traffickers?"

"Yeah. He wants to meet up with a guy in Tampa. Apparently, he was on the ship last night. Said he saw Jack and me, and more importantly he says he saw what happened to the boat we were chasing."

"You want me to come with?"

"There shouldn't be any trouble."

"I've heard that before."

I thought for a moment. "What about Scarlett?"

She nodded. "Fine. I'll stay. But I better not find out that you got into another fight without me. Who's going to save you if I'm not there?"

Ange has saved my butt more times than I can remember. And she rarely passes up an opportunity to remind me.

It took me a while to fall asleep. There was a lot on my mind. When I finally did sleep, it felt like my eyes closed for mere seconds before I woke up just after 0700. Ange and Scarlett were still asleep. I kissed Ange on the forehead, got ready, then drove over to the airport to meet Scott.

FOURTEEN

Angelina woke up to the sound of the Tacoma's engine and the sun bleeding in through the cracks between the curtains. Scarlett woke up minutes later to the smell of coffee, and the two had strawberry-banana-mango smoothies for breakfast. After playing with Atticus in the yard, Ange ran her through a quick yoga routine.

As they finished up, she got a message from Jack.

"Still up for bug roundup?" it said.

Ange looked over at Scarlett. She was drenched in sweat and collapsed onto the hammock.

"Hey, Scar, you feel like catching lobster this morning? I figured since it's your last day and—"

"Yes!" she exclaimed. She swung around and jumped to her feet. "I'd love to."

Her fatigue went away in an instant, and if her excitement was swayed in any way by the dark clouds on the eastern horizon, she didn't let it show.

They were soon ready and headed outside when they heard Jack pull his blue Wrangler into the driveway. Once at the marina, they loaded up on the *Calypso* and Jack motored them out of the harbor. Just as they reached one of Jack's secret honey holes, it began to rain. Thunder grumbled. Strikes of lightning pierced the cloud-covered sky.

"Don't worry," Lauren said. "If you don't like the weather in the Keys, just wait a few minutes."

Jack didn't complain. In fact, he relished whatever mood his island paradise was in. Rains and thunder meant poorer visibility and therefore less competition out on the water. And the lobsters knew it too. They were more daring when the weather was bad. More willing to venture out from the safety of their hiding places.

Taking cover in the saloon, they gave Scarlett a quick demonstration after dropping and setting the anchor.

"Finding the good ones is the tricky part," Jack explained. "Catching them is simple—if you know the technique." He grabbed a metal rod. "This is a tickle stick. Now all you gotta do is fin up close to the antennas. Then, while holding the net out behind them, you tickle their front. Their instincts kick in, they book it backward, and they swoosh right into your net. Dinner's served."

Scarlett's enthusiasm grew with Jack's animated presentation.

"Are we scuba diving like yesterday?" she asked.

"Freediving," Jack said with a grin. "It's more challenging, but also more rewarding."

"We're only over about thirty feet of water," Ange said. "Plus we'll show you the proper techniques."

They did. Within half an hour Scarlett was able to

reach the bottom with one breath. Being properly weighted and using long freediving fins, she was amazed at how fast and effortlessly she could move through the water.

Once ready to go hunting, Jack pointed toward a limestone outcropping with a row of antennas sticking out.

"It's all yours," he said.

They were treading water on the surface. He handed her a tickle stick and Ange handed her a net. She'd already donned the gloves.

She was ready to go.

A deep breath, a smooth kick to raise her up in the water, then a duck dive down into the clear tropical ocean. She reached the bottom in just a few seconds, equalizing the pressure on the way down. When she reached the outcropping, she stabilized herself, then moved in.

With the net in position, she reached with the stick and tapped one of the lobsters. Just as Jack had said, the bug kicked backward in a flash. The unsuspecting creature swam ferociously straight into her net. She smiled big, then looked up. Ange and Jack were peering down from the surface. They both gave her a thumbs-up and she ascended toward them.

She cheered as she broke the surface and raised her no-longer-empty net up out of the water.

"No need to measure that one," Jack said with a grin as he climbed up onto the swim platform and grabbed hold of the net.

He dropped the bug into the live well, then handed the net back to Scarlett.

"After catching your breath, you want another go?" Ange said.

It was as rhetorical as a question could get.

"I want a hundred more goes."

They spent another hour in the water, watching each other dive and taking turns going down to fill up their coolers. They scouted out a few more sites and managed to get some of the biggest lobster Ange had seen in the Keys. Even after they'd bagged their limits for the day and their hands looked like prunes, Scarlett kept wanting to go down.

Jack convinced her to climb out when he fired up the grill.

"You think they're fun to catch," he said, "well, they're just as fun to eat."

Just as the grill was warming up and they were preparing a handful of bugs to be cooked, the cockpit radio crackled to life.

"This is *Aquaholic* hailing Sea Ray," a man's voice said.

Jack paused a moment. He didn't recognize the name. He glanced at Ange and Scarlett, then shuffled up to the pilothouse and grabbed the radio.

"You can start up on those," he leaned down and said to Ange.

She nodded and continued seasoning the tails.

"This is *Calypso*, go ahead."

"I'm dead in the water about a mile southwest of you," the guy said. He had a thick Australian accent. "Something wrong with the engine. Can't say more as this is my first time taking her out on the water. Do you happen to know anything about boat engines, mate? I can pay for the help. I'd just as soon not get the Coast Guard involved."

Jack understood. He'd never had to call in the Guard for boat trouble in all his years on the water. Better to handle it on your own if you can.

Or phone in a friend, I guess.

"Is your anchor dropped?" Jack said.

There was a short pause.

"Should it be?"

Jack rolled his eyes.

Some people just shouldn't be out on the water alone.

"You're floating in the Florida Current, man. Roughly three knots right now. That means you'll be far out into the Straits in a few hours. Not bad fishing out there, but given your situation, yeah, I suggest you drop and set your anchor."

"Right," the voice replied. "I'll drop it right away."

"Good."

Jack brought up the radar. He saw a few echoes, but only one was within a mile of them. Grabbing a pair of binoculars, he focused out over to the port bow, facing southwest. The boat was small in the distance, but he guessed that it was a thirty-foot Regal.

"Alright," Jack said into the radio. "I'm heading over. ETA five minutes."

"Thank you. I really appreciate it."

Jack set the radio on the dash and turned around.

"Hate to cut our lunch short," Jack said, looking down to where the girls were dropping the first lobsters on the grill. "We've got King Landlubber supposedly dead in the water."

"That's okay," Scarlett replied. "We can just cook in the galley."

"First do you mind doing me a solid and heading up to the bow and—"

"Releasing the safety lanyard?" she said, springing around the pilothouse and onto the bow. "I got you covered."

Jack grinned, then glanced over at Ange.

"I thought you said yesterday was her first day on a boat?"

Ange shrugged. "It was. Maybe she has conch in her blood or something."

Jack brought up the anchor, and the girls migrated into the galley as he fired up the engines.

FIFTEEN

The weather turned foul again as they motored toward the *Aquaholic*. Rain fell in thick sheets. Thunder roared like Thor was having a temper tantrum, and lightning flashed across the sky.

On the ride over, Jack tried to imagine what the guy he had spoken to looked like based on his voice and predicament. Tall. Too much cologne. Designer sunglasses.

And he's Australian, so probably a blue flag with a Union Jack in the canton blowing in the wind.

He chuckled as the image appeared in his mind.

It wasn't that he had a problem with people wanting to get into the boating lifestyle. Far from it. He encouraged it and made his living off those kinds of people. But it was the ones who set off without so much as reading a boaters' manual or making basic attempts to understand how their boats worked that ground his gears.

Boating is great, when done correctly, he thought.

As he motored closer, he caught his first clear glimpse of the boat through the rain-splattered windscreen. He'd been right. It was a Regal. Twenty-nine feet long. And it looked like a new model, its hull painted a shiny blue with a white stripe parallel to the waterline.

It was a nice boat. Probably put the owner back well over a hundred grand. Not the kind of boat you want to take out if you don't know what you're doing.

As Jack motored closer, he spotted a big guy standing at the stern beside a pair of Yamaha 200-hp outboards. He had a toolbox open on the seat beside him and a dark blue Bimini top open to keep him relatively dry, though the rain had already abated significantly.

"Ahoy, mate," the guy said in a strong Australian accent.

He waved to Jack, who was piloting from up in the flybridge. Jack's mental image of what the guy would look like and the real thing were eerily similar. He was tall, with blond hair, wide shoulders, and a silver cross earring in his left ear. He wore pristine designer clothes, and though Jack was too far away to tell, he was certain he'd have on too much cologne.

Jack waved back as cordially as he could fake it. He eased down to just a few knots while Scarlett and Ange tossed a pair of fenders over the side. Once the Regal was tied off, Jack idled, then killed the *Calypso*'s engines.

The guy's demeanor shifted when he laid eyes on the girls.

"You ladies having a nice time out on the water?" he asked.

Scarlett did her best to suppress chuckling at the

guy's goofy suave behavior.

"We were," Ange fired back. "What's wrong with your boat?"

The guy smiled.

"Well, I was hoping you could help me with that. I'm more used to a boardroom than a boat." He stepped over and held out a hand. "I'm Flynn."

Jack reached the main deck and strode between the girls and their new landlubber acquaintance.

"Jack," he said, shaking the guy's oversized hand. "Permission to come aboard, Flynn?"

The big guy's smile broadened. "Please, be my guest, Jack."

Jack sprang over.

Three for three, he thought, catching a whiff of the guy's musky cologne. *Well, no Australian flag. Three for four isn't bad.*

The rain had died down to just a drizzle, but the deck and engines were damp. Jack knelt beside the two outboards. They looked pristine. Practically brand-new. No rust, discoloration, or visible defects.

"You said this was your first time piloting her?" Jack said while kneeling into a crevice for a better look.

"Yeah. It was my great-uncle's boat. He left it to me in his will. I live in Orlando. Just down for a few days. Figured I'd take her for a cruise out to Dry Tortugas. I've never been and heard it's beautiful."

"It is," Jack said. "And you're alone?"

"Yeah, mate."

Jack went through his usual hierarchy of boat engine troubleshooting. Starting with the most common problems, he worked his way down.

Was there gas? Was there oil? Were the engines being properly cooled? Yes on all three counts.

"Go ahead and try starting them up," Jack said.

Flynn nodded, moved into the cockpit, and tried the key. Nothing. Not even an abnormal noise. That cleared it in Jack's mind.

"It's gotta be electrical, man," he said. "When was the last time it was taken out?"

He stared back at Jack blankly.

"I'm not sure. As I said, my uncle—"

"Did you have it checked before you came out today?" Jack already knew the answer to his question.

"No, mate."

"You got the paperwork on her? The last inspection date should be there."

Flynn stared back at him confused for a few seconds, then said, "Alright, I'll check in the cabin."

He stepped out of view. Jack shook his head.

This guy's either high as a kite or he doesn't have two brain cells to rub together.

He checked the electrical connection to the engines. No problems there. The battery and spark plugs checked out as well.

He grabbed a wrench from the toolbox and stepped to the cockpit. He'd have to take apart the paneling and work his way through the components one at a time.

"You find the problem, mate?" Flynn said from down in the cabin.

"Soon as I do, you'll be the first to know, man."

Flynn stepped up into view. Jack kept his head down, working a bolt loose with the wrench.

"Hey, Flynn, you mind—"

Jack froze when he heard footsteps, then saw two more guys appear from the cabin.

What the hell? He said that he was al—

Flynn reached for a handgun barely visible under

106

the right side of his shirt.

A blood-chilling realization came over him. These weren't down-on-their-luck tourists. There was nothing wrong with the engine. And they didn't need help. Jack had been hailed over with the radio for a different reason. A far less law-abiding one.

"Jack?" Ange said from over on the *Calypso*. "Everything alright?"

No time to answer. Jack was quick, but the three guys had the upper hand. And the numbers.

In a rapid movement, Jack swung the wrench toward Flynn's left knee. But before he could strike it, the closest new guy tackled him hard to the deck. He was much shorter than Flynn, but strong. He and Jack tumbled into the bottom of the dashboard. Somehow Jack still managed to maintain his grip on the wrench.

Just as he was about to slam it into the guy's face, he heard an unmistakable click.

"Move and I'll blow your head off," Flynn said, his tone migrating from helpless landlubber to ruthless criminal in an instant.

SIXTEEN

Ange didn't hesitate. She pushed Scarlett out of harm's way and lunged for her backpack. It was resting against the starboard gunwale and had her Glock inside it.

"Hold it right there, miss!" the third thug yelled as he aimed his Makarov handgun straight at her. He was just as big as Flynn but had dark skin and wore a black tank top.

Ange froze in her tracks. She was standing right over her backpack, debating what to do, and Tank Top could see the conflict in her eyes.

The short guy who'd tackled Jack from behind jerked the wrench from his hands, then grabbed him by his tee shirt and jerked him to his feet. He grabbed a handgun and pressed it against the side of Jack's head.

As Ange was about to drop for her Glock, Tank Top intervened. Aiming his Makarov straight at her in his right hand, he moved up against the port gunwale. Then he reached into his pocket and pulled out a small metal orb. It took less than a second for Ange and Jack to realize what it was.

A grenade.

He quickly pulled the pin and held it out over the *Calypso*'s deck.

"One more move and I'll drop it," he said, staring straight at Ange.

Ange swallowed hard.

"Best not test him," Flynn said confidently. "He has a short fuse."

For a few seconds, the group remained frozen. Ange's eyes scanned from Tank Top to Flynn to Jack.

"I'm a reasonable man," Flynn continued. "I follow a strict philosophy of minimal collateral damage. It's what's best for business. All I want is the girl. You give her back to us, and none of you will be hurt."

"The hell with that," Ange fired back. "You try and take her and it'll be the last thing you'll ever do."

Flynn smiled, then chuckled emphatically.

"You're either the bravest or the stupidest Sheila I've ever met," he said. "Let me spell this out for you. There are three of us and we're all armed. You try and make a move and we'll riddle you all with bullets. You try and kill us, and he'll drop the grenade and it'll blow up right in your lap."

Ange wasn't intimidated. She knew that she could take all three of them. But she needed her Glock to do it. The one that was resting in her backpack a knee bend and an arm's reach away from her.

She ran through scenarios like a computer. How long it would take her to snatch it up and take aim. She could do it. She could get them out of this mess.

But what about Jack? He had a pistol pressed to his temple. She needed to communicate with him somehow. She needed to get him on board with her plan.

"Stop!" Scarlett said suddenly. She held her hands in the air and stepped toward the starboard side of the *Calypso*. "I don't want either of you getting hurt. I'll go." She looked up at Tank Top, then at Flynn, and said it again. "I'll go."

She glanced over her shoulder at Ange. Her eyes were teary but focused.

"I'm sorry," she mouthed, then turned and stepped over the gunwale.

"No!" Ange said.

Flynn nearly pulled the trigger.

"Not another step!" he snarled at Ange. "You," he said, directing his gaze to Scarlett, "over, now!"

Flynn stepped beside Tank Top at the port gunwale, grabbed Scarlett forcefully, and pulled her onto the Regal.

Ange made eye contact with Jack. She nodded to him slightly, and he nodded back. This was it. They'd need to act quickly and with perfect timing if they were going to have a chance at this.

Jack made the first move.

With only one guy holding him down, he managed to rip an arm free, jerk his body around, and grab hold of Shorty's wrist. Shorty pulled the trigger just as Jack forced the barrel off his head. A round exploded from the chamber like lightning, firing straight into the overcast afternoon sky.

Flynn glanced away from Ange toward the commotion at his back. It was only a split second, but it was long enough.

Ange dove for her Glock. Clasping it with her

right hand, she rolled to the side as Flynn fired off a barrage of rounds that flew right over her head. She managed to stabilize herself, take aim, and get a shot off before Flynn got her back in his sights.

Her 9mm round tore through Tank Top's left thigh, causing him to lurch forward and grunt. Ange had hoped he'd fall into the space between the boats, but he managed to stay on his feet, his grenade still in his hand.

Scarlett jumped into action. She slammed a heel into Flynn's left foot, then elbowed him in the gut. He grunted, then smacked her hard across the face.

Jack broke Shorty's wrist and knocked him to the deck. The short, muscular thug reared back and yelled violently as he retaliated with a powerful front kick. Jack's wiry frame flew backward, crashing into Tank Top and causing both of them to roll over the sides and slam onto the deck of the *Calypso*.

Tank Top dropped his handgun, and Ange watched with wide eyes as the grenade fell from his grasp as well. It hit the deck in slow motion and rolled straight toward her at the port gunwale.

She might've had time to toss it away, but where? She couldn't throw it onto their enemy's boat. No, Scarlett was there.

With no time to think, her body took over. She and Jack both lunged for the port side, then dove headlong as far as they could and splashed into the water. Just as their bodies broke through the surface, the grenade exploded.

A loud boom. A powerful rumble. And a release of razor-sharp shrapnel in all directions.

Tank Top was barely able to stagger to his feet before his body was ripped to bloody shreds. What was left of him flew back, smashing against the transom, toppling onto the swim platform, and splashing into the water. The sliding glass door shattered. Pieces of the deck broke apart. A plume of smoke rose above the boat.

The explosion resonated through the water. Even muffled by the *Calypso*, it still shook Ange and Jack as they turned over and headed back for the surface. Bursting out of the water, they could hear the loud groan of engines. It was the Regal. Flynn and Shorty had dropped to the deck and were unscathed. They had Scarlett and they were already making a break for it.

Both Ange and Jack reached for the top of the port gunwale and pulled themselves up in one quick motion. Ange rolled onto the deck, snatched her Glock, and took aim. She fired off three rounds in succession, one striking Shorty in the shoulder before they grabbed Scarlett for cover and turned out of view beyond the bow of the *Calypso*.

Ange didn't skip a beat. With the agility of a cat, she practically sprinted around the cockpit and onto the forward tip of the bow. Planting her feet, she raised her Glock again. This time, she wasn't aiming for the cockpit. She couldn't risk hitting Scarlett. Instead, she aimed for the engines, hoping to disable the craft or at the very least slow their escape.

She fired over and over, relentlessly raining lead upon the rapidly escaping boat. Despite her efforts, the Regal continued to creep farther and farther from her grasp.

Soon, her Glock clicked and the slide locked back, signaling that the magazine was empty. She kept her eyes locked on the boat, as if her surging rage could stop it in its wake. Her jaw clenched tighter and her gaze narrowed as the boat grew smaller and smaller in the distance. Her anger and resolve intensified with every passing second. Her breathing was quick, her eyes focused.

Soon, the Regal was nothing but a blip on the southern horizon.

When Ange finally lowered her weapon, she realized that her hands were shaking. Her hands had never shaken like that before. She'd been thrown into danger against overwhelming odds time and time again in her life. She'd fought, killed, and narrowly escaped death's grasp. But her hands had never shaken.

Seeing the boat motor from view and not being able to do anything about it cast cold, hard emotions upon her that she'd rarely felt before. She could only watch as the boat disappeared. She could only watch as they took Scarlett.

"Ange!" Jack called out from the cockpit.

It was the fourth time Jack had called her name in the past thirty seconds, but she'd only heard the last one. She was so focused, so entranced by her anger, that her mind had blocked out everything else.

She snapped out of it. Spinning around, she saw Jack standing with the radio in his right hand.

"I'm getting ahold of the Guard," he stated. "You need to call Logan."

She nodded but remained frozen in place for a few seconds before fully snapping out of it and climbing back around and onto the deck.

SEVENTEEN

The helicopter touched down at the Port of Tampa an hour and a half after taking off at Key West International. The pilot brought us down in a field just north of the main cargo shipping facility. When the rotors slowed and the door opened, Scott and I stepped out behind two members of his security detail.

He'd given me a rundown of the situation during the flight. We'd be meeting with a ship crewmember who wished to remain anonymous. He was going to give us intel on what had happened to the boat that had disappeared in the Gulf. He gave his name but asked for discretion for the sake of his job. After researching him, Scott and the CIA deputy director had learned that he'd been working for various cargo ship companies for over ten years.

Despite the matter being well below his paygrade, Scott wanted to talk to the guy himself. Unlike most politicians, he was a man of action and liked getting his hands dirty. Just the way he was wired. And he'd asked me to tag along, given that I'd watched the scene unfold a few nights prior.

I wore a pair of cargo shorts, a gray tee shirt, and tennis shoes. Scott wore his usual well-fitted suit, though he'd left the jacket in the helicopter. Good looking, well built, and as sharp as they come, Scott was one of the most badass guys I'd ever met. Not many Rhodes Scholars make the decision to turn down lucrative financial opportunities in exchange for the rigorous life of a Navy SEAL. But Scott thrived on challenges, both academic and physical.

With the wind still billowing down from the main rotor, we stepped out onto the grass. We'd flown in a Sikorsky VH-3D Sea King, the same make and model used by the president, and it was painted dark blue and white.

A man wearing a white hard hat and a gray dress shirt tucked into jeans met with us briefly and pointed us in the right direction.

The main section of container traffic is along the western shoreline of East Bay Chanel, a narrow strip of deep water that connects East Bay and Hillsborough Bay. It handles over thirty million tons of cargo every year, goods transported primarily to and from Central America and the Caribbean, and the port covers a surface area of over five thousand acres. It's also the closest US port to the Panama Canal, giving it a strategic advantage in the maritime shipping industry.

We stepped through a checkpoint, then moved into the cargo holding area. There were rows of various brightly colored shipping containers, many stacked up to four high. Once we entered, we could see nothing but walls of metal on both sides, with the occasional break. Even though it was still early, the place was already loud with activity. Two freighters were tied off. Massive cranes lifted shipping containers off one, stacking them on the shore.

The man we were there to talk to was going to meet us right in the middle, on the shaded side of row E. We reached the spot a few minutes early. There was nobody around, no movement as far as we could see in either direction.

Scott and I got to talking about the whole thing while waiting.

"There's just something I can't wrap my head around," he said. "Why would the billionaires that run these operations jeopardize everything by trafficking women?"

I didn't have to think that one over to come up with a response.

"You deal with the rich and powerful all the time," I said. "You know how many of them think. Like they're above the law. Hell, many of them are. And when you're above the law, you feel like you can get away with anything. What did you guys find on the freighter?"

"It's an independent. Gets contracted out by various shipping companies."

"Somebody must own it."

"A shell conglomerate apparently," he said.

"And at the top?"

"We're working on it. But there's a lot to sift through."

I shook my head. It was some shitshow. I found it hard to believe that a sex-trafficking operation existed on at least one shipping freighter without the head honchos who ran the show knowing about it. Which

116

meant that we might be dipping our toes into a massive highly illegal and morally corrupt operation.

I glanced at my watch. Our contact was five minutes late.

Growing impatient, Scott grabbed his cellphone and quickly called an already stored number. He waited for thirty seconds as it rang and rang and rang. No answer. He tried a second time. No answer again.

We stood for a few more minutes before a vibrating phone caused us to go quiet. But it wasn't Scott's phone. It was mine.

I reached into my pocket and pulled it out. It was Ange. The screen showed a picture that I'd taken of her in Curacao a few months earlier.

I pressed the answer button and held it up to my ear.

"Hey, how—"

"Logan, they took her," she said, cutting me off. She was frantic, her words rushed.

My heart stopped. "What? What do—"

"They took Scarlett," she gasped.

EIGHTEEN

We were halfway back to the helicopter by the time we ended the call. Pocketing my phone, we sprinted the rest of the way to the chopper, then Scott told the pilot to take off.

Ange's words resonated in my mind.

Attacked. Firefight. Scarlett abducted.

Ange was alright. So was Jack. But a group of guys with guns had taken Scarlett, and they were motoring south, into the Straits of Florida.

My heart pounded as I stared with a narrowed gaze through one of the side windows. The pilot had us up and flying back toward Key West in a blur.

After questioning me as much as I'd questioned Ange, Scott went to work. He called contact after contact, starting with the commanding Coast Guard and Navy officers in the Lower Keys.

I wished I hadn't left. I wished I'd been with them. Ange is one of the best mercenaries on the planet, and

Jack can hold his own much better than most. Whoever had managed to swipe Scarlett and get away with their lives couldn't have been novices.

There never was a damn contact, I thought, the fact creeping into my mind. *The entire thing was a ruse to get me out of their hair.*

The burning anger I felt transformed into a firm resolve.

Wherever they take her—to the ends of the earth, to the darkest, most dangerous depths—I will find her. I will bring those who took her to justice, and I will bring her to safety.

Ten minutes after takeoff, Scott got a call back from Wilson.

"We can't find a boat matching the description via satellite," Wilson said, his voice all business over the speakerphone. "We've swept the area over and over."

"What about a freighter?" I said, looking over at Scott. "Any of those between Key West and Cuba?"

He paused a moment then went back to work.

"There's one," he said after a few minutes. "It's heading for Havana. Should reach Cuban waters in the next half hour."

Wilson sent over the info on the freighter. It was larger than the one they'd tracked two nights earlier and was owned by a different company.

I thanked him for the intel and told him I'd be in touch.

After ending the call with Wilson, we sat in silence for a few seconds. My gaze was narrowed as I stared out the nearby window.

"You've got a look in your eye I've seen before, Dodge," Scott said. "I sure hope you're not about to do what I think you're about to do."

My gaze shifted to meet his. I didn't need to

answer that question. He already knew the answer.

"You barely know her," he added. "Let us handle this."

"I'm going to find her, Scott. That's all there is to it."

He paused for a moment, then sighed.

"There's talk of the president going to Cuba. He even wants to eventually lift the travel ban. But we're a long, long way from that. You go there and you're on your own. We can't have your back there. No one will."

"I'm not expecting any help."

Scott turned and looked me dead in the eye.

"They'll kill you, Logan," he stated. "You start meddling in their business and they'll throw everything they've got at you. These are big-time criminals and it's their home turf."

"I don't give a shit how big-time they are. Or how many there are or where we engage. I'm going after them and I'm going to bring her back. Because that's what a man does when injustice knocks on his fucking door. A man stands up."

Scott shook his head.

"Don't preach to me about injustice and how men ought to deal with it. I fought these bastards in the muddy trenches with you for years and now I'm fighting them behind a desk. There's a right way to handle this and there's a wrong way. Who benefits if you get yourself killed?"

We fell silent. Only the choppy whir of the rotor blades and the occasional sounds of radios from the cockpit filled the air.

He was probably right. He had always been much smarter than I was. The logical move would be to follow his plan and to play by the rules of the legal systems. But I couldn't get her out of my mind. The picture of Scarlett being taken, beaten, drugged, and worse was all I could see. I'd only known her for a few days, but that had been enough. I was going and there was nothing Scott could say that would stop me.

"How in the hell do you plan on getting there anyway?" Scott said. "How do you think they knew she was on the *Calypso*? They knew the boat, and that means they also know yours."

"I guess we'll just have to find an alternate form of transportation."

"You better not be thinking about flying. You're too smart to even think about flying a private—"

"One way or another, we'll get there."

I stood, strode to the cockpit, and asked for an ETA.

"Five minutes," the pilot said without taking his eyes from the sky in front of him.

I moved back and plopped back down. Scott had watched my every move, but I stared forward. My mind was made up, and he knew it.

We lowered in altitude and soon we were on the tarmac. Back in Key West.

I rose to my feet. The door couldn't open fast enough. I strode for the steps as soon as I could.

"Look, Logan," Scott said, stopping me at the door. "I'll keep in touch. We've got everyone we can mobilized on this, but once they reach Cuban waters there's not much we can do."

"I know," was all I said.

"Just… be careful, alright? Make the first move and don't give these guys an inch."

I nodded and headed down the steps. Ange was sitting in my Tacoma right on the tarmac, engine running. She stepped out and I wrapped my arms

121

around her.

Wind from the chopper roared against us as it took off. I held her tight for a few seconds, then got a good look at her.

"I'm fine," she said.

Her eyes were focused. They stared back into mine, mirroring my own resolve.

"I'm sorry," she said. "I'm—"

I held a finger up to her lips. "This isn't your fault." I looked up at the truck, then added, "Let's go."

Nothing more needed to be said. We were both on the same page. There was no point in asking her not to come. That would be wasted breath. Besides, as much as I wanted to keep her safe, I needed her by my side. Scott wasn't messing around or just trying to scare me. We were about to walk willingly into a damned lion's den.

We hopped into the truck and I hit the gas.

NINETEEN

I drove us over to our house, pulling into the driveway at just after 1100. I killed the engine and we headed inside. I went straight for our safe in the master bedroom closet. After punching in the code and pressing my thumb against the biometric scanner, I pulled it open.

I packed an extra Sig for myself and an extra Glock for Ange, along with stacks of untraceable ammunition for both. I also grabbed my M4 carbine assault rifle, Ange's collapsible .338 Lapua sniper rifle, two bulletproof vests, a small case of throwing knives, and a case filled with my favorite intel gathering electronics.

Scott had used to call it saddling up back in the SEALs. Looking over the impressive amount of firepower, I realized that it had been a long time since I'd saddled up to that extent. But going against a powerful sex-trafficking ring, we'd need all the help we could carry.

We had a small special section within the safe. A section we rarely touched. Remnants of our past lives as mercenaries when we'd often had to sneak into countries and infiltrate operations without drawing attention. I grabbed a fake Canadian passport for each of us from a stack. I also grabbed a few wads of Cuban Convertible Pesos, or CUC as they're referred to. Though Cuba has two main currencies, the CUC is the one most used by tourists.

Once I had everything I needed, I loaded it all up into narrow watertight hard-shell cases. We filled a waterproof backpack with extra clothes and tactical gear, then loaded everything into the truck.

On the drive over to the marina, I asked Ange where Jack was.

"He's tugging the *Calypso* to Queen Anne's Boatyard," Ange said. "The deck got blown to hell by the grenade, and the engines are shot. He's taking it for repairs."

Queen Anne's Boatyard. That gives me an idea.

"The old fishing trawler still over there on the hard?"

"Far as I know." Ange paused a moment, then glanced at me and nodded. "I'll give Nick a call."

She quickly got ahold of Nick Alto, the owner of Queen Anne's, and after he verified that the trawler was still there, Ange asked how long before he could get it in the water and ready to go.

"Half an hour," he replied.

"Do it," Ange said. "We'll cover any costs when we get there."

After hanging up, she turned to me.

"Looks like we've got transportation," she said.

At the marina, we boarded the Baia and loaded up

124

two sets of rebreather gear, along with our fins and masks, into a cart. We also loaded up two sea scooters, underwater flashlights, and drysuits. Once we had everything we needed, I locked up the Baia and turned on the security system.

We carted our stuff to my truck, loaded it up, then took off out of the city.

It took us an hour to drive from Key West to Queen Anne's Salvage in Marathon. It was a nice place, with a boat launch, rows of boat storage racks, and a twenty-foot-deep channel. Nick had been running the operation for years and had inherited the business from his dad.

I parked the truck in the small dirt-and-sand lot. We walked toward the water and spotted Nick just as they were lowering the trawler into the water. He motioned toward the trawler, then yelled that he'd be right in the office. Just out over the water, I spotted the *Calypso* being towed toward the dock.

Instead of waiting in the office, we walked over and offered a hand with the straps after the trawler was lowered.

"Thanks for getting her in on such short notice, Nick," I said as we offered our assistance. "Any word on what's gonna happen with her?"

Nick was average height and well built. He always wore cargo shorts and flip-flops and always had on a dirty old tee shirt and sunglasses with a strap.

"I got no problem holding on to her until the government decides what they're gonna do," he said. "Providing they keep sending the checks." He looked over the trawler, then added, "She sure is a strange boat. I've never seen anything like her in thirty years of examining thousands of crafts."

He was right. The trawler had originally been

constructed by a private military group called Darkwater. Though a rusted and decrepit hunk of metal by all appearances, the trawler had some of the most advanced electronics on earth. And it had two 800-hp Mercruiser engines that could push the heavy craft through the water at up to forty knots.

I'd first encountered it when I was attacked by a Russian Darkwater assassin in Cay Sal Bank in the Bahamas. After me and an old Navy buddy dealt with the guy and his posse, the government had taken possession of the trawler. It had been at Queen Anne's ever since, only going out on a few occasions when we required its particular blend of speed, advanced electronics, and ambiguity.

The *Calypso* was pulled toward the dock. Jack was standing up in the flybridge, but he climbed down and tossed me a few lines to pull him over beside the trawler. He was wearing nothing but a pair of board shorts and seemed quiet and sullen, nothing like his usual laid-back persona.

I climbed onto the *Calypso* and pulled him aside.

"You alright?" I asked, taking a look at the damage.

The main deck was cut and torn, the windows shattered to pieces. There was a burn mark crater in the center of the white deck.

"I'm fine," he said. He took in a deep breath, then sighed. "They find the boat?"

I shook my head.

"That's what we're gonna do."

He nodded.

As we tied the *Calypso* off, Nick strode over and froze in his tracks when he saw the damage.

"Jackie, what did you do this time?" he asked as Jack hopped onto the dock.

"A grenade blew up on the deck," he replied flatly.

He clearly wasn't in the mood for beating around the bush.

Nick stared blankly for a few seconds.

"Dare I ask how in the hell that happened?"

Jack went quiet, then handed Nick the keys and said, "Bit of a long story. Do me a favor and call me when you have an estimate."

After Nick pocketed the keys, Jack walked over to us near the base of the dock.

"You're not gonna stay?" Nick said, raising his eyebrows. "Usually you won't let someone so much as clean the windows of your pride and joy without you looking over their shoulder."

"Any other time I would, man. But we've got something we need to do."

"Gonna go after the ones who threw the grenade?" When we were silent for a few seconds, he raised his hands in the air. "None of my business. I get it. I'll send you a quote later this afternoon."

Jack nodded. "Thanks, Nick."

Nick motioned toward the trawler and added, "She's ready to go. Keys are on the dash."

Jack helped us haul the gear onto the trawler. We checked a few things in the cockpit and engine room to make sure that the vessel was seaworthy. As Nick had said, she was in good order, topped off and ready to go.

I started up the massive 800-hp engines and powered on the electronics, and we cast off the lines. Once we'd moved away from the dock and into the channel, I handed control over to Jack.

"Do we have a heading?" he asked.

"I'm gonna check in with the guys," I replied. "Havana for the time being."

He nodded and punched in the destination.

I sat alongside Ange at the table. She already had the laptop open and was researching shipping ports in and around Havana. My phone vibrated in my pocket just as I was about to grab it. It was Wilson over at the CIA. I put it on speakerphone and answered.

"The freighter pulled into Havana Harbor," he said. "Looks like it's tying off in Casablanca, a ward on the northern shore of the harbor. I'll send you the coordinates."

"Did you continue scanning the straits?" I asked. "Just in case you missed the boat the first time around."

"We did. But we're confident that this is the escape vessel. Especially after the incident you were involved in the other night. I've called a few of my contacts in Cuba and we're trying to work out how to go about handling this."

"Well, be sure and let me know how your talks go," I said.

He paused a moment. "Uh-huh. And where are you?"

"Just taking a little boat trip."

He sighed. "Look, I'm sure Scott told you everything already, so I won't regurgitate it. Just know that the guys pulling the strings at the top of this thing are multibillionaires. You know the level of power that kind of money can buy, especially in places like Cuba."

"Got it," I said. "Thanks for the intel."

"Just remember your priorities, Logan. The endgame here is putting a halt to a sex-trafficking ring. Not just saving one girl."

No, Wilson. You're wrong about that. The endgame for me is both. Two birds with one stone.

A moment after ending the call, Wilson sent us the latitudes and longitudes of where the cargo ship docked. I gave them to Ange while Jack piloted us south into Vaca Key Cut, under US-1, and into the Atlantic.

"I've got the location up," Ange said, staring at the laptop screen. "It looks like some kind of auxiliary shipping station. Maybe even a place for repairs. Relatively off the beaten path, looks like."

Off the beaten path is good.

She walked over and punched the coordinates into the trawler's GPS. Once set, she turned and sat back down beside me.

"Bringing her up to full speed," Jack said.

He slid the throttles forward and the big boat accelerated with ease. Within seconds we were cruising through the water at forty knots.

"ETA in two and a half hours," Jack said.

TWENTY

Two hours into the voyage, I stepped out onto the bow for some fresh air. It was 1400. The sun was hanging high, but I couldn't see anything except its outer glow through the veil of clouds. Thunder rumbled in the distance. The rain had subsided, but the dark clouds up ahead promised a return.

Ange joined me. She walked up with two mugs of coffee, handed me one, then looked out over the water. Though severely overcast and windy due to our speed, it was still warm. The occasional spray of seawater up over the bow felt good.

"I'm not leaving Cuba without her, Logan," Ange said after taking a sip.

I glanced over at her, then nodded.

We'd only known her for two days, but the time had made an impact. Ange had already looked into adopting her. In her mind, I could tell, she was already ours. Our responsibility. Potentially, one day, our daughter. As hard as it is to believe, I felt the same way.

The cockpit side door opened and Jack stepped out.

"We're twenty-five miles out," he said. "Soon we'll be getting hailed with questions. What's the plan here, bro? Cuba isn't exactly the warm neighbor down the street who brings you fresh muffins. They protect and surveil their waters like hawks."

"If they ask what we're doing, just make something up," I said. "Then once you drop us off, you apologize and haul ass out of there."

"Drop you off? Are you crazy, bro? This is a foreign country, and a communist one at that. They'll be waiting at the dock before we reach the shore."

"Who said anything about dropping us off on the shore?" I said.

Twenty minutes later, when we were roughly ten miles north of the harbor, a Cuban Naval patrol boat hailed us asking to state our business. Ange and I had already put our drysuits on over our clothes and were prepping all of our gear at the stern.

We grabbed our cases and the waterproof backpack, then started up our rebreathers. Using the rebreathers would allow us a longer bottom time than scuba. Also, being a closed-loop system, we wouldn't have to worry about bubbles rising to the surface and giving away our position. When it comes to being stealth underwater, nothing beats a rebreather, and I'd been using them for years, both in the SEALs and many times after.

We were almost finished getting our gear ready when Jack hopped out from the cockpit.

"We've got a patrol boat incoming," he said. "Three miles out and closing in fast."

131

Keeping calm and collected, Ange and I picked up the pace and moved everything to the stern. We needed to get into the water fast, but moving frantically and getting our heart rates up wouldn't solve anything.

Smooth is fast. Fast is smooth.

Jack eased the throttles back to fifteen knots, then carried the sea scooters to the stern.

"Eight miles, south-southeast," he said, answering my question before I'd even had a chance to ask it.

I ran the quick calculations in my head. The sea scooters could pull us through the water at a max speed of seven knots. But we'd be slower due to the drag of our gear. Figure maybe five for the easy math. That meant it would take us roughly two hours to reach our destination inside the harbor. The upgraded batteries in the sea scooters could last two and a half hours at full speed. It was cutting it close, but we could always kick the rest of the way if one of them died early. The rebreathers would give us over three hours, so time wasn't an issue with them.

We secured the rebreathers, strapped our gear to the harness, then donned our full facemasks and fins. Jack handed us each a sea scooter and gave us a laid-back salute.

"Go get those assholes," he said.

Jack didn't curse often, so when he did, he really meant it.

I peeked over the port bow and could see the customs boat closing in. It was less than a mile away. I gave Jack a fist bump, then nodded to Ange.

"You reading me?" I said, testing the face mask radios.

"Loud and clear."

We shuffled to the transom and turned around,

sitting on top of it. After one more glance at each other, I gave Ange a thumbs-up, then dropped backward into the white bubbly wake of the trawler.

I spun and twisted and sank in the chaotic haze of the churning water. After a few seconds of going with the dizzying flow, I slowed to a stop and was able to take in my surroundings. I looked up, then glanced at my dive computer. I was ten feet down.

Aside from Ange and the wake of the trawler above, there was nothing.

Diving far out in the open ocean, where there's nothing for miles and endless blue beneath you, can be a daunting experience. With Jack motoring the trawler away from us, we were alone. If our equipment malfunctioned or if we were somehow spotted, we'd be forced to improvise and make do on our own.

"Time to get deeper," I said, motioning a thumb down while looking at Ange.

She nodded and we both descended to thirty feet.

"You all good?" I asked.

"Never better. Nothing like falling into a blender."

We powered up our sea scooters, then oriented ourselves using compasses attached to our wrists. We had dive flashlights, but there was no sense in using them. The near-perfect viz allowed the glowing sunlight to illuminate the water around us.

Once ready, we flattened our bodies and held on as we started up the propellers and accelerated through the water. Once up to speed, all we had to worry about was ensuring we were on course and maintaining our depth. I took intermittent glances up toward the surface but knew that someone had a better chance of winning the lottery than spotting us from a boat.

To pass the time, I played songs in my head. "Bad Boys" kept popping into my mental playlist, and I sang the occasional line, which caused Ange to chuckle and then join in. To help get myself into the proper mental state, I also thought about Scarlett. I thought about how scared she was and what I was going to do to the guys who had taken her when I found them.

"We're nearing the mouth of the harbor," Ange said.

I didn't need a GPS to know that she was right. The clear ocean shifted to a brown haze within just a few minutes. Boat traffic increased, mostly small-hulled pleasure craft.

Visibility dropped dramatically as we entered the Canal de Entrada, a thousand-foot-wide, forty-foot-deep channel that connects the Port of Havana to the ocean. Not wanting to be smashed by a passing ship or churned up in its wake, we moved to within just a few hundred feet of the shore and ascended to twenty feet down.

If we'd been on the surface, we would've been able to see the Castillo San Salvador de la Punta off to the right and Castillo de los Tres Reyes del Morro off to the left, two impressive stone fortresses that had protected the city for hundreds of years.

We motored toward the shore of the Peninsula de Belot and surfaced under a long wooden dock. Based on the map we'd surveyed and the intel from Wilson, the freighter we were looking for was just a few hundred yards to the east of that current position.

Staying together, we switched off the sea scooters and rose slowly. We surfaced in the shade of the dock and had about three feet of clearance between our heads and the planks. The dock was old and rustic, the support beams covered in thick layers of barnacles and grime.

To our right, we could see the bottom half of a freighter. Ange lowered her mask, finned a few kicks toward it, then nodded.

"That's the one," she said. "It's right where Wilson said it'd be."

I moved beside her and examined the vessel. Roughly five hundred feet long, it appeared relatively new and was filled to half capacity based on its waterline markings. There was no activity aboard or on the pier beside it.

Directing my gaze away from the freighter, I looked for a place where we could get out and remove our gear without drawing suspicion. A hundred feet down the dock, I spotted an old sailboat that was wrecked beyond repair but still managing to stay afloat. With no sign of anyone on it or nearby, we decided it would suit our purpose nicely.

We swam around to the other side and took another look around, then I climbed up onto the stern. Setting my sea scooter and rebreather aside, I bent down and helped Ange up behind me. We didn't need to break the lock on the saloon door. It swung lifelessly on its rusted hinge. Moving inside, we pulled off our drysuits, then stashed our dive gear.

"Alright," I said to myself as I stepped into the tiny head and checked myself in the mirror.

We'd made it into Cuba. Now it was time to find Scarlett and punish those who had taken her. Again, the bad boys song played in my head, and I wondered if it would be stuck there all day.

"Logan," Ange said quietly.

I stepped back into the saloon. Ange had moved topside, her head sticking down through the small door.

Seeing the serious and somewhat relieved expression on her face, I said, "What is it? Do you see her?"

"Not exactly," she replied. She motioned for me to follow her, then added, "You gotta see this, though."

I headed topside and saw her standing on the starboard side, facing the freighter and peering through a small pair of binoculars.

I gazed where she was looking and saw someone walking down the pier toward the shore. Whoever it was, they were far off, but it was clearly a male.

I stepped toward Ange and she handed me the binos. I peered through and put the guy in the crosshairs. A bell went off in my head the moment I looked at him. It was his gait and clothing that gave him away more than anything else. A slight limp, bright colorful tee shirt. Funny hat and sunglasses.

"It's that punk from Pete's the other night," Ange said, taking the words right out of my mouth.

I watched him intently as he strode with awkward confidence to the base of the pier. I could see him clearly in my mind's eye. Sitting at Pete's, checking out Scarlett and then groping her as she passed by. Scarlett had taken him down and taught him a lesson, or so I'd thought.

Duke. That was his name. That was what Mia had told me back at the restaurant.

"It sure as hell isn't a coincidence," Ange said. "Seeing him at Pete's, and now seeing him here."

"No, it isn't," I said, still watching the guy like a hawk. "He knows where Scarlett is."

He was almost to the base of the pier and we didn't want to lose him. We slid on some shades to better conceal our faces, then dropped down onto the creaky dock. We left our dive gear and sea scooters concealed on the old sailboat, taking only my waterproof backpack and the hard case with our extra firepower.

There were only a few people on the dock. Two old fishermen who looked like they'd been trying their luck at that spot since Castro and his revolutionaries had overthrown Batista. There was also a guy in the water scraping the algae and barnacles off a small fishing boat's hull, and a guy fixing up an old Balboa sailboat. None of them seemed the least bit concerned by us.

Why would they be?

We probably looked like a couple of lost tourists, or maybe a couple looking to buy and fix up an old boat. They didn't care.

We kept our eyes glued on Duke, watching his every movement and interaction, and we soon reached the shore. Moments later, the guy disappeared from view between a row of old buildings.

We kept our distance, keeping a solid bead on him as he weaved through a maze of old warehouses. Soon, he headed toward a rundown dive bar and shoved his way through the solid black doors.

There was a guy in an adjacent alley smoking. A few classic American cars lined the quiet street. Graffiti covered most of the visible walls. It was dingy and looked like it had never been repainted. All in all, it looked about as shady as the grass under a sycamore tree.

"This place looks promising," Ange said.

I smiled. "You mind if I do the honors? I could use a drink."

She shrugged. "I guess so. I'll be ready to move in

137

once I hear bottles shattering. Or if this punk does the smart thing and decides to make a run for it."

I gave her the backpack, strode across the street, and pushed my way through the door.

TWENTY-ONE

Somehow, the place looked even worse on the inside. Even "rustic, neglected dive bar" was too glamorous a description.

It was like in those old western movies when the mysterious out-of-towner steps into the local bar. All eyes gravitated toward me as I quickly scanned the room.

The place reeked of mold and sweaty clothes. An old TV in the corner displayed the static image of a soccer game, while a radio in the opposite corner played Spanish music. There was a pool table that had more craters on its green felt surface than the moon, and a wooden dartboard that looked like it had been pummeled by a shotgun for half an hour. It was dark inside, the few lightbulbs that did work flickering and dying out.

I counted ten people in all, including the old waitress and the fat guy behind the bar. Most of the patrons were seated at tables playing poker in the space between empty beer bottles. None of them were Duke.

There was a door beside the bar, and another one across the room. There was also an old staircase that looked like it didn't get much traffic.

With no visual on my target, I decided to wait, figuring he'd gone into the head to relieve himself before blowing his black market profits on booze and whatever else this guy spent his money on.

A new hat, maybe.

I chuckled.

More than a few pairs of questioning eyes stared in my direction as I navigated across the room and leaned against the bar.

"I'll take a rum, neat," I said when the bartender's eyes met mine.

He paused a moment. After a brief skeptical look, he shrugged, finished wiping down a glass with a rag, then turned and went to work. The counter was scratched, chipped, and faded to hell. The whole place looked like a relic of a time long gone by.

I glanced around the room again. Not as many people were looking at me, but I caught the occasional side glance over the shoulder or around a hand of cards. I was a stranger. An outsider in their little world. Most of them could've been normal ship crew, not even associated with the crime syndicate. But they sure gave off the criminal vibe.

The fat bartender turned around and set my drink in front of me. No napkin first.

Why bother?

He watched intently as I grabbed the glass.

I was sure by his smile that he'd given me his strongest stuff. Well over the typical eighty proof. He was trying to find out what I was made of.

Pressing the glass to my lips, I tilted my head back, then dumped the contents down the hatch in one long pull. The alcohol burned as it flowed down my throat.

Easily over a hundred proof.

I set the glass back on the counter. It wasn't half bad.

The fat guy paused only long enough to see my reaction, then said, "Another?"

I smiled at his obvious disappointment, then nodded.

"There are fifty bars between here and downtown," he said as he turned around to fix me up round two. "Why'd you walk into here?"

His voice was raspy, his English good.

"I'm looking for someone," I said, stopping him in his husky tracks. He turned back, eying me skeptically. "His name's Duke. Young guy. White. Dresses like a sideshow clown. Ring any bells?"

He stepped toward me, wiped the counter with his dirty rag, then leaned in closer.

"You looking for a girl?" he asked, not bothering to lower his voice.

It didn't matter. Not in that joint.

"Yeah," I replied.

He smiled. "You might wanna try the Malecón after ten. Hell, you could try it at any time these days."

"I'm looking for a particular girl."

He paused a moment. "Doesn't work like that here, boss. Not unless you got some real deep pockets."

I narrowed my gaze. "Do you know where Duke is or not?"

He chuckled. I caught a foul whiff of his breath and nearly gagged. "You know, you're pretty ballsy for an outsider." He leaned over, looked me up and down. Sizing me up. "Duke's not here. Last I heard he was in Haiti. Tough luck, buddy."

Now it was my turn to lean in closer.

"I know the punk's here," I said sternly. "Tell me where he is and you won't have to visit the emergency room today."

It wasn't my best threat, but it was the first one that came to me.

The fat guy chuckled again, then leaned back and stood tall.

"You threaten one of us, outsider," he bellowed, "and you threaten all of us."

It was like the record scratching and going silent in old movies. Chairs kicked back and fell. The guys around the room rose to their feet in unison. Hands clenched into fists. And every pair of eyes in the place bore into my back.

A fight with a bunch of rough-looking criminals in an old and grimy dive bar. Does it get any more clichéd than that?

I didn't care. Even if they did have one hell of a home court advantage. I'd take them all on right then and there if I needed to.

I eyed the fat guy and began planning out my strategy to engage when I spotted something that caught me off guard. Through the reflection in my glass, I caught a glimpse of something colorful. It was out of place in the grungy, muted bar.

I snapped my head sideways and looked up. It was Duke. He was standing against the second-story railing, peering down at me. It was a quick glance. Just long enough for me to see his face display a powerful blend of fear and surprise.

The guy was still wearing his big-rimmed purple sunglasses. He lowered them, along with his jaw, in perfect synchronization.

Before I could turn the rest of my body around, he was gone. Like a spooked lobster after you tap it with a tickle stick. He turned on his heel and took off out of sight.

I glanced down toward the rest of the guys in the bar. I wanted nothing more than to take them all down like Patrick Swayze in *Roadhouse*. But Duke was my mission.

Instead of running after him and being inevitably roadblocked by a row of his friends, I kept still and started a mental stopwatch.

One thousand one... one thousand two...

Calmly, I turned around and faced the bar.

"At least let me finish my drink," I said, eyeing the fat guy.

One thousand five.

I grabbed the glass, leaned toward the bartender, and splashed it into his face. Whirling around, I grabbed hold of the wooden stool beside me and threw it at the two closest guys who were moving in on me.

One thousand seven.

Then I darted to my left and sprinted out the back door to a chorus of cursing and yelling.

One thousand ten.

Ten-second head start for Duke. It wouldn't be near enough.

Glass bottles shattered against the door behind me as the guys inside ran after me and threw whatever they could get their hands on. The guy smoking in the alley glanced up from his phone and stared at me. I looked skyward, heard footsteps, then spotted Duke sprinting along the rooftop of the dive.

Wanting to get out of there before his intoxicated merry men stormed out, I took off down the alley as fast as I could.

Their yells shook the still afternoon air as they slammed the door open far behind me and stormed out.

I didn't look back. I pumped my arms, sprinting as fast as I could.

Ange must know something's up. She's probably heading down on the other side to cut him off.

I took intermittent glances up as I bolted to the other side of the row of structures. Duke had a nice lead at first, but I cut it in half as he jumped from one rooftop to another, then dropped down out of view.

Just as I rounded a corner, I watched as he slid down the fire escape and jumped into the passenger side of an idling 1950s Impala. The driver hit the gas, causing the tires to scream and spit out smoke as it accelerated away from me.

Unable to catch them on foot, I grabbed my Sig and took aim. I only managed a single shot, shattering the rear window before the driver peeled out of view down a cross street.

I lowered my weapon.

Shit. Ange, where are you? Where the hell are you?

The thought that maybe she'd been hurt or captured entered my mind for a second before I heard the sound of a second engine and screeching tires. A red 1951 Buick convertible flew around the corner and braked to a stop in front of me. I smiled when I realized it was Ange in the driver's seat.

"Get in," she said, peering at me through her dark

aviator sunglasses.

I slid over the hood and jumped into the passenger seat, not bothering with the door. The moment my rear hit the classic red-and-white leather seat, Ange floored the gas pedal. The classic engine groaned and forced me against the seat back. We accelerated quickly, and she shifted like a pro from gear to gear, then barely slowed as she swung a right turn.

"There they are," I said, pointing ahead.

The Impala was barreling down the side street, braking only to turn a sharp left onto a busier street.

"I see them," Ange fired back, shifting into third gear and maintaining our high speed throughout the turn.

The driver of the Impala was good, but Ange was better. She quickly closed the gap to less than fifty feet. Looking ahead, I saw that we were rapidly approaching a busy intersection.

The driver didn't hesitate. He braked, then turned sharply, weaving right between a flatbed truck and a guy on a moped. The momentum caused the car to ride up on its two left tires, nearly flipping before the driver managed to stabilize it.

Ange followed suit, hitting the corner with better precision and coming into formation right behind the truck.

She stomped on the gas, and I held on as she brought us up over eighty miles per hour.

We needed to close in and make our move soon. They had home field advantage. They'd also probably called in backup already, shortening our window of opportunity. We had one lead in the whole country, and we were going to make the guy talk come hell or high water.

"Looks like we got a jam up ahead," Ange said

over the roaring engine and billowing wind.

Roughly a quarter of a mile ahead of us, the traffic was stopped and backed up a handful of vehicles. I spotted glimpses of bright orange vests, heavy machinery, and handheld traffic signs. Construction.

This was it. There was no turnoff or street between us and the closest stopped car. Our quarry had nowhere to go.

With my Sig still in hand, I prepared to hop out and engage them once we stopped. Just before they reached the line of stopped cars, they cut a hard right, driving right off the road. One of the workers yelled out for them to stop, but it was useless. The driver accelerated, smashing the car through a row of duranta bushes and a short wooden fence.

Ange kept right on them. She turned sharply, the tires skidding along the pavement and onto the dirt shoulder. We drove right through the hole their Impala had made, bouncing over the flattened shrubs and shattered remnants of the fence.

We followed right behind them, chasing them down at over fifty miles per hour through a field of scattered cows. I spotted Duke as he looked out the passenger side window. He peered at us, then extended out an arm that was clasping what looked like a revolver.

This is my cue.

I rose up in my seat and took aim with my Sig. I didn't want to kill him. I wanted to stop their car.

I put the rear left tire in my sights and fired off two rounds. The tire exploded, causing the car to jerk sideways and skid out of control. We were approaching another fence, this one barbed wire, and what looked like a drop-off beyond.

I fired off another round, this one into the rear

window to force Duke to take cover. Once he was back in the car, I blew the other rear tire as well. The car slid wildly back and forth, then shook violently as it slammed into a large boulder.

It performed a fast full-360-degree turn, crashed through the barbed-wire fence, and flew out of sight over the edge. Ange slammed on the brakes, grinding us to a stop less than ten feet away from the drop-off.

I shoved open my door, threw my backpack over my shoulder, grabbed the hard case, and took off with Ange by my side. We sprinted to the edge, then froze when we realized how steep it was. It was a sheer drop of at least thirty feet. The Impala had been smashed to pieces. It was upside down and resting in a small muddy stream below.

We moved along the rim to a more welcoming gradient, then slid down the dirty slope on our butts, knocking a few loose rocks and causing them to tumble down in front of us. When we reached the bottom, we took a look around. There was nothing nearby except a distant barn and a few curious sheep.

I set my backpack and the hard case aside, then we both splashed into the water and grabbed hold of the frame of what looked more like a smashed-up tin can than a car. If anyone inside had survived the fall, they'd be too messed up to move. Especially in that old vehicle. The thing most likely didn't even have seat belts, let alone modern safety features like airbags.

There were only two bodies inside. The driver was sprawled out, his left leg twisted awkwardly and his face covered in blood. Duke was also motionless. He lay facedown against the roof. I reached in through the shattered driver's-side window to feel for a pulse. He was dead.

Shit.

"Well, there goes our lead," I said.

Ange crawled in on the other side, careful not to cut herself on the shattered glass.

"Maybe," she said, "maybe not."

She searched Duke's pockets. A gold-and-white-striped pack of cigarettes. Two condoms. Some loose pocket change. Useless random trinkets. Then held up a cellphone.

I smiled. "That'll work."

We shimmied out of the battered car and took two steps back across the murky stream before we heard the unmistakable sound of sirens. They weren't far. Probably less than a mile.

We both looked up at the steep precipice, then turned around.

It's time to ditch our vehicle.

I glanced down at the cellphone.

And figure out who this guy Duke's been talking to.

TWENTY-TWO

Ange and I ran across the field, taking cover behind a row of bushes, then around the back side of the old barn. Once out of sight, we continued down a dirt path to the end of the farm. We hailed a cab at the Rotonda de Cojimar, a large roundabout with palm trees in the middle.

The driver hopped out of his classic white Ford Fairlane beside the curb and opened the door for us with a ready smile. When he asked where we were heading, Ange took the lead.

"Take us to Old Town," she said.

He shut the door behind us, hopped into the driver's seat, then took off around the Rotonda and onto the Via Blanca toward downtown. The closer we came to the heart of the city, the more the unique and authentic feel of the Cuban culture took over. Our enthusiastic driver pointed out attractions and historical sites as we passed by. He clearly loved his country and spoke of its rich history and world-renowned hospitality.

He also told us about Old Havana: where we had to eat, what we had to see, what to avoid. He also told us that we'd arrived right in the middle of the Carnival de la Habana, the annual vibrant carnival, which was going to kick into full swing later that afternoon.

He also explained that Old Havana was centered around five main plazas and that it has some of the most beautiful architecture in all of the Americas. The architecture, the classic vehicles, and the overall vibe when we entered Old Town made me feel like I'd gone back in time fifty years.

The driver's laid-back and warm personality was a nice change of pace from the tensioned exchange in the bar and the fast and furious chase that had welcomed us to the country.

I gazed through the partly open window as mopeds revved chaotically. Locals chatted on steps. People coming and going out of businesses tucked in stairwells.

I'd read before that Cubans are some of the friendliest people on earth. Meeting the driver and looking at all the people as we passed by, it was easy to see how they'd garnered that reputation.

He dropped us off in front of Café Bohemia, along the southwestern edge of the Plaza Vieja. He explained that it had once been the main plaza in Havana and that it had been restored to look much like it had when it was originally laid out in 1559.

We paid and thanked him, then stepped out.

The plaza was beautiful. With ripples of intricate archways lining the lower levels of the surrounding buildings. Roughly an acre of smooth cobblestone, and an ornate fountain in the center. Small potted trees. A nice ocean breeze sweeping in from over the rooftops. A cat sleeping on a shaded ledge. A blend of various conversations, and the occasional distant honking car horn. Nearly every window from the second floor and up was accompanied by a small balcony with flowerpots.

A curious well-behaved dog trotted up and smelled me briefly. I petted him for a few seconds before he carried on about his day.

"There's a bed-and-breakfast up there," our driver said, pointing above a nearby café.

The upper part of the building he pointed at had classic windows with bright blue shutters. Looked nice, but also inconspicuous.

He smiled and waved, then drove off down the cobblestone street.

We headed for the café. Moving past a sea of tables with white umbrellas, we entered between two large support columns covered in flowering ivy.

Before giving in to our grumbling stomachs, we headed upstairs to book a room for the night. We were both too anxious to check Duke's phone to eat. Being the rainy season, we had no trouble securing what the woman in charge called her favorite room. It was easy to see why. It was simple, but fresh and clean. And it had a large window and a balcony with a small table and chairs that overlooked the entire plaza. From up there, we could even see peekaboo views of the waterfront a few blocks away.

We paid in cash, using our fake IDs, and the friendly woman handed us the keys. When she was gone, I locked the door and set my backpack as well as the hard case on the bed. Ange and I sat beside each other on a small colorful couch. She pulled

Duke's phone from his pocket, and I grabbed my backpack and unzipped the small compartment.

Inside, I grabbed a small pen recorder/radio transceiver. I also grabbed a specialty hacking device that had been developed by an old friend of mine named Murph. The genius computer wizard had given me the device years back as a reward for saving his life when he'd fallen into dangerous hands. There was nothing else like it in the world—a handheld device that could be used to track the location of any cellphone during an active call.

Ange went to the contacts first, a short endeavor given that there weren't any.

"Burner phone," she said.

I nodded, half expecting that.

She then went to the recent activity. There were a handful of sporadic calls spread out over the past three days. Ange started with the most recent, pressed the call button, then turned on the speakerphone.

I pressed record on my pen, wanting to catch every word of whoever answered. I also powered on the hacking device. But no one answered. After two rings, the line went dead. Ange tried again. Same result.

Scanning down, she tried the next three most recent calls. Nothing.

Ange was growing frustrated, and so was I. We weren't exactly overflowing with leads. If Duke's phone turned out to be a dead end, that meant we'd have to go back to the drawing board. It also most likely meant another trip to the dive bar over at the shipyard, where we'd have to fight our way to getting answers that might not even be there.

"They must know he's been compromised," Ange said.

It was a strong possibility. I glanced at my dive watch. It was half past five. That meant it had been about thirty minutes since Duke and his buddy had gone head-to-head with gravity and lost big-time. That's a long time in the age of cellphones and the internet. Word of what had happened could have easily traveled all throughout their operation at that point. Since Duke was dead, that would mean they'd most likely block or ignore calls from his number.

Ange continued, trying a handful more before sighing and shaking her head. I was just about to rise to my feet and recommend lunch when a voice came over the small speaker, replacing the familiar pendulum drone of the ringing sound.

"What the hell do you want?" a rough masculine voice answered.

It was faint, but it sounded like the guy had an Australian accent.

I glanced at Ange, whose mouth had dropped open.

"Hello?" the guy barked. "Are you there, dickhead?"

There was a strange sound in the background. Sounded like metal clanging against metal. Distant music as well. And a few muffled male voices.

Ange and I looked at each other, then at the hacking device hooked up to the phone. It was working. It wasn't like in the old police movies. We didn't need to keep the line alive for a certain amount of time. The device could hack into the cell tower faster than we could say "*está volao*."

It was a good thing too. A moment later, the guy hung up and the line went dead.

"What's going on?" I asked, leaning closer to Ange.

She shook her head, then thought for a second.

"I know that voice," she said. "That guy was on the boat back in the Keys. He was one of the guys who took Scarlett."

TWENTY-THREE

"I'm sure of it, Logan," Ange said. "He sounds exactly the same."

I never doubted for a second whether she was right or not. Ange had great hearing and even better attention to subtle details when it came to people's mannerisms.

She thought for a moment, then a lightbulb went off in her head.

"Flynn. That was his name."

Ange leaned back into her chair and I watched as the hacking device did its job. Less than a minute after the call ended, the small LCD display gave us the guy's coordinates. I grabbed my laptop and brought up a GPS. After quickly punching in the series of numbers, I pressed enter. The map of the world zoomed in on Cuba, then on the Miramar district, and pinned the guy's position.

"He's on Avenida Forty-Seven," I said. "Two

buildings south from the intersection with Forty-Nine Bravo."

Ange performed a quick online search.

"It's a gym," she said.

I nodded.

"That would explain the noises in the background."

"It's called Gimnasio de Toros. Looks like it's a pretty small place. Not much of an online presence."

I brought up our location relative to the gym and saw that we were roughly four miles northeast from it. Or about a fifteen-minute cab ride.

I glanced at my watch. It was nearly 1800 and we'd had quite the day already. My stomach was grumbling, but the meal would have to wait. Trails can get cold quick. In my experience, if you have an opportunity, you need to nab it as fast as you can. In other words: strike while the iron's hot.

Taking our phones, wallets, and handguns, we stashed my backpack and the hard case in the closet, then locked up and headed back downstairs. We moved into the warm, humid early-afternoon air of the plaza. Most of the people were sitting in shaded areas around the perimeter or taking pictures in front of the fountain.

Two blocks west, we hailed a cab and told the driver to take us to El Bosque. It was a forest park along the Almendares River, just down the street from our real destination. A couple of foreigners dressed in casual clothes and asking a cab driver to take them to a gym wouldn't add up. It would certainly be outside the norm, and we didn't want to do anything that looked outside the norm.

We drove through the bustling downtown streets, our driver utilizing side roads, and reached our destination a few minutes under the GPS estimated time. After stepping out at the forest, we waited a few seconds for him to drive off. The park was beautiful, tall trees covered in bright green vines. The sounds of the distant flowing river filling the air.

Once the cab disappeared around a corner, we turned around and walked east out of the park and along a sidewalk. The gym was across the street and half a block away.

We moved past a few food cart vendors and took our first look at the place. It was small and slightly rundown, but not nearly as decrepit as the bar I'd walked into earlier that afternoon. It blended into its surroundings well, nestled between a bakery on one side and a narrow alley and a nail salon on the other. There were a few cars parked along the curb, but I assumed that there must be a parking lot nearby.

We took a leisurely lap around the block to scope out the place and to make sure that we weren't being followed. Once back near the entrance, I switched on my pen transceiver and slid it into my back pocket. Ange would be listening in via a small radio with an earpiece.

We decided it was best that I take the lead again, given the fact that the guy who'd helped snatch Scarlett would probably recognize her. On the drive over, she'd given me a description of him. Tall, wide shoulders, short blond hair, blue eyes, a silver cross earring dangling from his left ear, and of course the Australian accent.

Once ready, I nodded to her, then turned and moved across the street. I pushed my way through the swinging front door and caught my first glimpse of the inside. It was bigger than I expected. A crowded room with a yellow rubber floor and scattered fitness machines from retro infomercials. The place smelled like dirty laundry.

I scanned the room but saw no one except an old guy wearing a baggy red tank top and a white headband and puffing a cigar while operating a noisy rowing machine. More than a little counterproductive.

I looked up at a few squeaking ceiling fans. In the back, I heard music, slamming weights, and low voices. The same sounds we'd heard in the background of the phone call. I only hoped that our guy Flynn hadn't called it a day yet.

I moved across the main room, through a partition, and into the back, following the sounds. In the rear were all the free weights. A long rack of dumbbells. Four power towers. And an Olympic lifting station.

There were four guys in there hitting the weights hard and nodding to the rock music. They were all big, muscular, and young. They also appeared to love showing off their muscles. I estimated that they might have enough fabric in all four of their tank tops combined to make a normal tee shirt.

Two of them were dark-skinned. Two of them were white but tanned. None of them were blond.

"Hey, are you lost, pal?" one of the guys said.

He was spotting a guy on the bench press and helped him rattle the heavy bar back into place after his set.

All four sets of eyes looked to me at his words.

"No," I replied.

I maintained my stride and scanned every inch of the room. There was an exit door in the back. A door to a bathroom or office to the right.

As I moved closer to the four guys, I noticed that they all had tattoos and visible scars. Something told me that they didn't make their livings as personal trainers.

"No?" the guy said, raising his thick black eyebrows.

"I'm not lost," I said flatly.

He rose to his feet, followed by the three others.

"What the hell is this moron's deal?" he said to his buddies in Spanish, thinking that I couldn't understand him.

He stepped toward me, got right in my face. He was a few inches taller and had about thirty pounds of muscle on me. Designer muscle, I hoped.

"If you're not lost, then what the hell are you doing here?" he spat.

"I'm looking for somebody."

The four guys paused, glanced at each other, then shook their heads.

Suddenly, I heard footsteps behind the closed door to my right. Then the door swung open on a squeaky hinge and a fifth guy stepped out with a cigarette in his mouth. He was big, like the others. Wide, muscular shoulders. Arms like most guys' necks. And blond hair.

Blond hair and a silver cross earring.

"Who the hell are you looking for?" the newly arrived bodybuilder said.

Australian accent.

"You. I think."

I fired off the response without skipping a beat.

He was taken aback by my response for only a fraction of a second. Then he tossed his half-burned cigarette aside, clenched his jaw, stormed toward me, and pointed a finger in my face.

"Look, asshole," he growled. "I don't know you. You come into my place and you act all suspicious. It's the kind of shit that really pisses me off. Now, tell me what the hell you want or me and my boys are gonna see how many forty-five-pound plates we can drop on your head before your skull crushes to pieces."

The four other guys closed in. They cracked their knuckles and necks, then narrowed their gazes at me.

"You met my wife," I said.

The Aussie shot me a sinister smirk, then chuckled as he glanced around at his buddies.

"I'm sorry, mate. Women are just attracted to—"

"Minimal collateral damage," I said, cutting him off. "That's your philosophy, right? That's what you told her anyway."

His eye twitched at my words. An obvious tell. If we were in Vegas at a poker table, I'd have already had him beat.

He looked confused for a few seconds, then tried his best to brush it aside and compose himself. It was too late. He'd already verified everything I needed to know. He was the guy from the phone, and one of the guys on the boat that had taken Scarlett. He'd made it clear without saying a word.

"Unfortunately for you," I continued, "we don't share that philosophy. When it comes to assholes like you, I'm more of a maximum collateral damage kind of guy. So, you've got two choices. You can tell me where she is and maybe you and your boys will get out of this with your miserable bodies relatively intact. Or, you don't tell me and I beat the shit out of all four of you right now in this smelly gym."

It was a lie, of course. Regardless of whether they said anything or not, they were all about to get the beating of their lifetimes. They just didn't know it yet. I never liked the taste of lies in my mouth. The only exception being when I said them to sorry

160

excuses for men like these.

The Aussie went from confused to laughing maniacally.

"You've got some big balls coming up in here," he said. "I don't know how you managed to track me down. Bravo. But it was all for nothing. You're never gonna see that girl again. That's just a fact, American."

"Tell me where she is," I said, raising my voice. "This is your last chance."

The guy laughed again.

He looked at his buddies and said, "Alright. Time to teach this guy a lesson. Then later we'll stuff his body into a wood chipper."

He motioned toward the doorway I'd entered from. The two metal doors slammed shut and were locked by the old guy I'd seen in the main room. He smiled and nodded back to the Aussie.

I was hoping to have Ange storm in and have my back. But it looked like a four-on-one fight was inevitable. Not the worst odds I'd ever faced. The only good thing was that since the bodybuilders all wore skintight clothing, I was able to see that none of them were armed. They were planning on beating me to a pulp with their knuckles.

A commercial over the radio in the corner ended and "Enter Sandman" began playing.

Fitting.

Suddenly, all four of them closed in on me. The white guy with the thick black eyebrows who I'd talked to at the beginning moved in ahead of the others. He was pissed off and clearly wanted dibs.

I wasn't about to rumble with this guy. If we went hit for hit, I was confident I could take him. But he'd mess me up in the process. Even if I managed to land

161

a perfect knockout punch to his face, the fragile tendons and bones in my hand wouldn't fare well. No, I had a different tactic in store.

In my peripherals, I could see that there was a power rack with a bar resting on it right behind me.

Always be mindful of your surroundings.

I could hear Liam Neeson saying the iconic words from *Batman Begins* in my head.

I took a step back. Reaching behind me, I grabbed the metal bar resting on the rack. Leaving the right side of the bar in place, I lifted the left side, brought it over my head, and swung it forward as fast as I could. Before the guy could react, the solid metal end slammed into his face, crunching bones and causing him to spit out a spray of blood as his head whipped sideways. He was lights out in an instant and collapsed to the floor.

A second guy lunged after me. The one wearing shiny sunglasses. I brought the bar back over my head and dropped it on the rack. Gripping tight, I dropped down, swung my body like a gymnast, and kicked him square in the chest with all the force I could muster. The air blew out from his lungs as his body curled and flew backward. He tumbled hard to the floor, then stabilized himself against a bench. Down, dazed, and injured, but not out yet.

The biggest guy in the group, a hulk of a man who looked like The Rock, came after me next. He threw a frenzied succession of left and right punches. I blocked and redirected them as best I could but took a strong blow to the shoulder that hurt like hell.

While I was dealing with the wild attack, the Aussie ran over and came at me from the side. He had a battle rope in his hands and tried to wrap it around my neck. Needing to make a move, I stomped a heel down onto the biggest guy's closest foot, then grabbed the Aussie's rope and used his own momentum to throw him to the floor.

By the time I turned back to the behemoth, he hit me with a strong front kick that launched me to the ground. I went with the blow as best I could, rolling under the power rack and coming to a stop on my hands and knees.

The massive guy yelled out, grabbed hold of the power rack, and grunted as he shoved the entire thing over. The heavy piece of workout equipment toppled toward me, and I just managed to roll out of the way before it squished me against the rubber floor. The metal bar rattled to the floor along with a stack of plates of various weights.

Looking up, I saw that the old guy was coming after me with a switchblade. Instinctively, I grabbed a five-pound plate from the floor beside me. Rising onto one knee, I hurled it toward the old guy. The solid metal struck him hard in the side, causing his body to spin and his hand to let go of the knife. He fell hard onto his back and groaned in pain.

Meanwhile, the biggest guy in the group had shuffled his big body around the fallen power rack and was zeroing in on me. He yelled as he bent down, trying to grab hold of me for his finishing move.

I reached back, pulled my dive knife from its sheath at the back of my waistband, and slashed his Achilles tendon. The ligament sprang up under his skin like a broken guitar string, and his leg gave out. The big guy shrieked as he fell onto his backside and reached for the damaged area.

I jumped to my feet and kicked him across the face, knocking him unconscious. The second guy I'd engaged, the one with the shades on, came at me from the right with a knife of his own. I reared back and threw mine through the air, lodging the blade center mass and stopping him in his tracks. He shook, blood flowing out and soaking his shirt, then collapsed.

That left only the Aussie.

He made his presence known in an instant with the cocking of a shotgun.

I spun around to look toward the sound. He was standing between the door into the main section and the bathroom. He had a blacked-out twelve-gauge aimed straight at me and looked angry as hell. His left index finger flexed on the trigger. The slightest bit more effort and a storm of lead pellets would burst toward me and shred my body to pieces.

He was staring right at me, about to speak when suddenly there was a distant mechanical sound.

In an instant, all the overhead lights shut off, sending the room into blackness. This was my chance, and I wasn't about to let it go to waste.

Darkness is a SEAL's best friend.

The moment the room went dark, I dove to my left as far as I could. I landed and reached for my Sig just as a powerful boom and a flash indicated a fired shotgun shell. I felt a sharp pain in my left leg but ignored it.

Just as I stabilized myself, the lights came back on. The Aussie looked spooked as I took aim and put a 9mm round into his left thigh. He fell to the floor, and I sprinted over and kicked the shotgun from his hands.

Banging erupted against the heavy doors behind me. I spun around with my Sig raised and saw Ange looking at me through the dirty window.

I put a round into the guy's right leg as well, just to make sure that he wouldn't move. He yelled and cursed me as I walked over to the door, unlocking it and swinging it open for Ange.

She stormed into the room with her Glock raised, then scanned every inch of it. We went around the room, making sure all our enemies were subdued and relieved of any weapons. I pulled my knife out of the chest of the guy who'd been wearing sunglasses, wiped the blood on his pants, and slid it back into its sheath.

"You had all the fun without me?" she said.

I shrugged.

"I had no choice. Thanks for cutting the lights. I'd be lying in pieces right now if you hadn't."

She holstered her Glock.

"That old guy locked me out just as I got to the doors," she said. "I was looking for a way to bust in when I saw the breaker panel." She looked me up and down, her eyes freezing when they reached the bottom part of my left leg. "Dodge, what the hell happened?"

She bent down, examining my left leg. I looked and noticed a circle of dark red at the bottom of my left calf, blood dripping down toward my sock.

"I guess I got hit," I said, remembering the sharp pain I'd felt just before I'd drawn my Sig.

In the heat of the moment, with my adrenaline pumping, I'd neglected to notice the wound. But once Ange had brought it to my attention, the pain resonated up my body. It wasn't a serious injury, but it hurt and it would require some attention.

I stepped across the room and grabbed a towel from a folded stack. Kneeling down, I wrapped it around my leg, but Ange stopped me.

"Let me do it," she said.

She knelt down, wrapped the towel carefully

around the wound, then tightened it to slow the bleeding. It was as makeshift as it gets but would have to do for the time being. We had important business to attend to.

"It's okay, Ange," I said. I motioned toward the Aussie. "We need to find out what he knows and get out of here before backup arrives."

She rose to her feet, and we turned our attention to the Aussie, who was sitting against the bathroom door, blood pooling beneath him. His half-burned cigarette lay on the floor beside him, letting off a thin line of smoke.

Ange bent down in front of him, stared him straight in the eye.

"You remember me?" she said. "I'm the girl that you never should have messed with."

Ange grabbed her Glock and slammed the grip into the guy's ear. He yelled out and gritted his teeth.

"Where's Scarlett?" she said.

I slid a forty-five-pound plate off a nearby rack and walked over.

"Remember when you mentioned how many drops it would take to crush a skull?" I said. "I'm thinking I'd rather start with your fingers. See how they hold up."

I pulled his left arm out, pinned it down with my foot and dangled the plate right over his hand.

He slouched his head down and panted for air. Shaking his head, he closed his eyes, then they sprang open.

"What the hell does it matter?" he said, struggling to get the words out through the pain. "We're... we're all dead now anyway. It's over. There's no coming back from this."

Ange and I looked at each other. We didn't say

166

anything. He was talking, and we wanted to see if he'd keep running his mouth.

"They took her to the Ranch, alright? That means it's already over. Your being here was all for nothing."

"The Ranch? Where is it?" I asked.

"I... I don't know where it is."

"Is it in Cuba?"

He shook as he nodded.

"What is it for?" Ange asked.

"It's a processing depot."

"What? Like a meat processing plant?"

He shook his head.

"It's not for processing animals. It's for processing women." He paused a moment, and we let him catch his breath. "Women from all over are taken there to be processed."

"Processed?" I asked.

I'd had enough experience with sex traffickers to know what that meant already.

"Better suited for slavery," he said. "The Ranch makes them submissive. By the time they leave the farm, they lose any desire to resist or fight back. They give in to their lot in life."

I glanced at my dive watch. He was lying, and by the look in Ange's eye, she knew it too. This guy knew where the Ranch was, but he wasn't going to tell us, and we were running out of chitchat time.

I dropped the metal plate right beside his hand, snatched my Sig, and aimed it at his forehead.

"Tell us where it is or you'll die right here right now," I said.

"It doesn't matter," he said between struggling breaths. He'd lost a lot of blood. "If you leave me alive, they will kill me anyway. You do not know our operation. You do not know the danger that you are both in now."

I squeezed the grip hard, then loosened and lowered it.

"Well, then, I guess I'll let them do the dirty work," I said, holstering my Sig.

"This is your last chance," Ange said. "Tell us where this Ranch is and we might be able to get you out of here."

He narrowed his gaze, then turned and looked away from us. We'd gotten everything we could out of him.

Ange stepped toward him and smashed her foot across his face, causing his neck to whip to the side and putting him to sleep.

TWENTY-FOUR

With all our enemies either dead or unconscious, it was time to get out of there. Before heading for the door, Ange searched the room and then moved into the adjoining office.

"Ange, we need to—"

"Not before I take care of that," she said, raising a first aid kit and pointing at my wound.

"It's just a scratch," I said.

She shook her head.

"No need to play tough guy with me. I know it hurts like hell."

I winced as she touched the towel.

"Alright," I said, grabbing her hand. "But let's put some distance between us and this place first."

She reluctantly agreed, and we slipped out the back door of the gym. Keeping a sharp eye out for reinforcements, we walked along a back alley for a block before reaching the parking lot. I made brief eye contact with a guy sitting in a black idling Chevy. I watched as he looked away from me, scratched his thick mustache, then lit up a cigarette. He looked... off. Slightly flustered.

I filed away the thought, then we cut a right, followed by a left into another alley that was empty aside from a few dumpsters.

We sat on the concrete steps at the side of what looked like an apartment building. Ange pried open the first aid kit and quickly went to work.

"Where do you think this Ranch is?" she asked, trying to take my mind off what she was doing as she carefully unwrapped the towel.

The blood hadn't dried yet, but it still stung. Especially when she doused it in antiseptic.

"No idea," I said. "And I doubt we'll hit anything but dead ends if we try searching for it."

"Ranch must just be their name for it. I'm sure it's not actually called that."

"Right."

I gasped as she moved in with the tweezers, grazing sensitive exposed flesh.

"Sorry," she said.

She was able to get the pellet, but if she'd been playing Operation, more than one buzzer would've gone off for sure.

With a smooth movement, she removed the bloody projectile and lifted it up.

"Souvenir to remember our trip?" she asked.

"I'd prefer a box of Cohibas," I said. "But only when the fat lady sings."

She dropped the pellet into a plastic bag, then finished cleaning the wound. Once it was ready, she stitched me up with the smooth and meticulous movements of a seamstress. When the stitches were in place, she ripped open a square Band-Aid and stuck it over the wound.

"Alright, well, it looks like you might get to keep your leg," she said as she helped me to my feet.

"Thanks to you and your breaker-opening abilities."

We tossed everything into the nearest dumpster, including the bag with the pellet in it, then took off down the alley. Less than a minute later, we turned right onto a busy street and hailed a cab.

"Take us to the best restaurant nearby," Ange said.

It was a good idea. As much as I wanted to stay hot on the trail and track down Scarlett as quickly as possible, we were running on fumes. Plus we needed to figure out where the Ranch was, and a good meal would help us think better.

A few minutes into the trip, the driver took us right past Havana's Revolution Plaza, the political heart of the country. Massive paved walkways surrounded by large buildings and monuments. Beyond the massive Palace of the Revolution, I spotted the star-shaped marble tower and statue erected in honor of the famous writer, Jose Marti, who'd advocated for independence from Spain.

Opposite the memorial are the offices of the ministries of the interior and communications, whose facades feature two matching steel memorials of arguably the most important heroes of the revolution: Che Guevara and Camilo Cienfuegos.

The driver stopped at the curb in front of a café, then leaned back to look at us both.

"Best ropa vieja in the city," he said. "Trust me, my friends, you will not want to leave."

We thanked him, handed him the fare along with a generous tip, then stepped out. The café was well

171

appointed, with gray suede seats, black hardwood tables, and a clean atmosphere. There was also an old piano beside the bar and a few classic bicycles up on the walls.

A well-dressed man greeted us, then ushered us to a spot two tables from the door along the side. The entire north-facing wall was open to air, putting the sights and sounds of the street life on full display.

Neither of us glanced at the menu. By the way the place smelled, we knew we couldn't go wrong. We each took the driver's advice and ordered a big plate of ropa vieja. To wash it down, we asked for a pitcher of water and two glasses of watermelon agua fresca. I also asked what else the place was known for, feeling more hungry than usual. I was surprised when the waiter said pizza and ordered one with sausage, pepperoni, and mushrooms to ensure I'd get full.

As we waited for our food, we looked out toward the street and leaned back to relax for a bit. The place was abuzz with activity. Everyday life in Havana in the rainy season. Looking around the restaurant, I only saw one other person sitting down, and he looked like he'd been there reading his newspaper all day.

It didn't take long for our food to arrive. We could smell it from the moment our waiter stepped out of the kitchen. He set down the two plates of ropa vieja, a traditional Cuban dish consisting of shredded braised beef, onions, peppers, olives, and a side of white rice. He told me that the pizza would be a few more minutes, and we both dug in.

It was delicious. Savory and flavorful tenderized meat that combined with the vegetables to create a taste that was both unique and incredibly enjoyable. By the time I was halfway through the pizza, I was toast and asked if he could box up the rest for me.

When we finished, we drank more to stay hydrated and began discussing the Ranch. Internet searches and forums produced nothing. I wasn't surprised. It was a very general term, after all.

What ranch?

That was the key question.

I thought back to the interaction with Flynn. I closed my eyes and replayed every word he'd said in my mind, hoping to find some kind of slip-up on his part. Then I stumbled upon it.

"Farm," I blurted out just as the word entered my mind.

"Farm?" Ange said, looking at me with confusion.

"Yeah. At one point, he used the word *farm* instead of *ranch*."

Ange chuckled. "Well, that really narrows it down. I'll just search for 'The Farm' instead and I'm sure we'll find our place. *Señor*," she said to our waiter. "*Cuántas granjas hay en Cuba?*"

The man looked caught off guard by the question. He stepped over, stroked his chin with a few fingers, then thought of an answer.

"*Muchas.*"

She thanked him and he walked off.

"Many farms in Cuba," she said.

I thought for a moment.

"What are the main exports from Cuba?" I asked Ange, who had her smartphone on the table.

She tapped the screen with her thumbs a few times.

"Sugar, tobacco, hard liquor, nickel mattes, crus—"

She paused, cutting off the last word. I could tell that she was mulling over something in her mind, and

173

I hoped she had something.

"Tobacco," she said quietly. Almost a whisper.

She closed her eyes for a few seconds, then opened them again. Leaning forward, she looked up and down the nearby street.

"Anything you want to share, babe?" I said.

She looked at me, then paused. Grabbing her phone, she ignored my question and tapped the screen a few more times. She was in the zone and trying to work something out. Having known her for nearly seven years, I was well acquainted with the look. It was best to just sit back and let her do her thing. Disturbances wouldn't help.

She looked up at me from her phone and said, "Come on, let's go."

We paid, thanked the waiter, then rose to our feet and headed down the street. After walking for half a minute, I noticed a black classic Chevy that caught my attention. It was identical to the one I'd seen idling in the parking lot back near the gym. This one had a guy leaning up against it with sunglasses on. He was trying to look inconspicuous. Trying a little too hard.

"We've got a tail," I said.

Ange scanned up and down the street. "Shit. The Borat-looking guy at ten o'clock?"

I nodded.

I kept a close eye on him in my peripherals while following Ange. We soon came upon a small corner store and I followed her as she headed straight for the tobacco section.

Her eyes scanned row after row of the packs behind the glass case. Then she settled on a brand in the middle and pointed her finger up to the glass.

"There you are," she said.

174

A worker opened the case and handed Ange her desired pack. Then we walked over to the cashier.

"Ange, don't tell me you're picking this habit up again?" I asked with a smile.

After paying, she pocketed the pack and we stepped outside. I glanced over my shoulder. The guy was still beside his car, and he'd turned to face our new position.

We continued down the street, then hopped in a cab. I was sure that the guy would be able to follow us but didn't care. I wanted to deal with one thing at a time. First, I wanted to know what was going on in Ange's head.

We settled in the backseat and gave the name of our bed-and-breakfast to the driver. He nodded and hit the gas. We were about ten minutes away, so we needed to use our time well.

I turned to look at Ange as she pulled the pack of cigarettes from her pocket.

"You don't recognize the label?" she said before I had a chance to ask another shot-in-the-dark question.

She handed me the pack. I opened it, pulled out one of the cigarettes, and examined it closely. They were all gray with thick parallel gold and white stripes. I was about to hand them back when an image appeared in my mind. I'd seen that same design less than an hour earlier. It had been half-burned and resting on the floor inside the gym beside Flynn.

"Flynn was smoking one of these," I said.

Ange's lips stretched to form a slight smile. "Yes. And Duke had been smoking the same brand. I saw it floating in the upturned car beside him."

I thought for a moment.

"So Flynn and Duke both smoke the same brand," I said. "I don't see the significance of that."

"These guys both smoke the same brand for the very same reason that you eat at Salty Pete's practically every day," she said. "Why pay for something when you can get it for free?"

"Hey, they serve some of the best food in the Keys, that's why."

She was right, though. Even though I offered to pay every time I went, I'm sure I wouldn't go quite as much if I knew they'd accept my offer.

"Well, let's go over what we know," she said. She eyed the driver, then lowered her voice. "We're looking for a farm. Tobacco is one of the largest exports in Cuba. And these guys both smoke the same obscure brand. You saw the shelf back at the store. This pack was one of maybe five like it and they were in the bottom corner of the section."

She had a good point. Certainly one worth looking into, especially given our lack of options.

"Let's see what we can find out about this farm," I said. I picked up the pack and read the label. "Gold N Ivory."

Ange nodded and went quickly to work. Within seconds, she found an information page.

"The farm is located in western Cuba," she began. Her eyes scanned a few lines, then she continued, "It is owned by…"

She froze, blinked a few times, then looked over at me.

I shrugged. "Who?"

She looked back at the screen, her mouth open. She'd officially grabbed all my interest.

"His name is Dante Salazar."

The name struck a chord deep within me. Back in the summer of 2008, just a few months after moving to the Keys, I'd stood between a helpless family and a

Cuban gang hell-bent on murdering them. The gang had been led by a notorious criminal named Benito Salazar.

"You know of Dante?" the driver said, waking me from my thoughts.

It was the first time he'd spoken since we'd entered the cab.

I came up with a quick answer and alibi.

"Never met him, if that's what you mean," I said. "We're with a Canadian missionary team. We're trying to help the victims of sex trafficking. This guy's name popped up."

I left it at that and waited. I'd merely mentioned the guy's name and sex trafficking. I wanted the driver to let us know if there was some kind of connection. Good or bad.

Over my years of traveling, I've found that cab drivers tend to know things about their cities that few others do. They see so much, driving around and giving people rides all day. And they communicate with their driver friends. If there was something going on at the Gold N Ivory tobacco farm, there was a good chance this guy knew something about it.

After about a minute without a reply, it was clear that he'd need some prodding.

"Is he related to the former gang leader Benito Salazar?" Ange asked.

It was the million-dollar question.

"He is nephew," the driver said. "Benito was a very bad man. Very hard, very bad. He kill many. When he die, the gang break apart. For a while, tensions were thick all over Cuba. Shootings and other violence were weekly news. But now things have settled, like ash after volcano eruption. The gang is now split, east and west. Dante runs the west half, as far as I know. Of course, some believe Benito is still alive. That he fake his death."

I couldn't help but smile at that.

There was no faked death. I'd killed Benito myself. His body was at that very moment chained under three hundred feet of ocean west of Dry Tortugas. Whatever was left of it anyway.

"And Dante's involved in sex trafficking?" Ange said.

The driver paused. He eyed us through the rearview mirror.

"I have already said too much," he sighed.

"No, it's okay," I said. "We're only here to help."

Without another word, he reached forward and clicked on the radio. A host's voice came on in Spanish, broadcasting a soccer game.

"I think it might rain later," he said, changing the subject faster than he changed lanes.

I shot Ange a sideways glance, then we both went quiet. A few seconds later, the driver pulled over in front of the hotel. We paid him, then hopped out.

"You know," he said, through the open passenger window, "you two don't look like missionaries."

He adjusted his sunglasses and drove off.

Glancing left, we both noticed that our tail had managed to keep up just fine. He was about fifty yards from us when he pulled over.

In sync, we turned and headed inside. Maybe he wasn't aware that we knew he was following us. If that was the case, we wanted to keep it that way.

TWENTY-FIVE

Dante Salazar stared down his assailant with the fiercest gaze in his arsenal. He held up his red-gloved hands at the last second, protecting his face from a barrage of jabs and uppercuts. His enemy was big, but Dante had fought much bigger. And he always came out on top.

At six feet tall, Dante had a rare combination of speed and strength. He had long black hair that he kept in a loose ponytail. He also had a thick beard and mustache. Much of his lean muscular body was covered in tattoos.

After blocking a hefty blow, he danced to the side, punched his assailant in the shoulder, then kicked him so hard in the side that he lurched and tumbled to the mat. Without a second's hesitation, Dante dropped and grabbed him from behind, putting him in a rear naked choke. The big Jamaican guy had no choice but to tap out.

He gasped desperately for air as Dante jumped to his feet. Reaching down a hand, he helped the big guy up, then patted him on his sweaty muscular back.

"The bigger they are," Dante joked between breaths, "the harder—"

"Rematch tomorrow, boss," the big Jamaican guy interrupted.

Dante eyed the big guy angrily. He lunged toward him and smacked him across the face with a powerful roundhouse kick. The guy flew off the mat and slammed hard onto his back, unconscious before he'd landed.

He stood over his conquered opponent, breathing heavily. He looked to a few of his gang members that were watching silently from the sides of the ring. He didn't say a word. Didn't need to. His point was loud and clear.

Nobody fucking interrupts me. Ever.

A middle-aged man wearing a polo shirt and a fedora handed Dante a towel and a full water bottle. Dante wiped the sweat from his face, then let the towel dangle over his shoulder as he quenched his thirst.

At thirty years old, Dante had been fighting since he could walk. His uncle had taken him under his wing, taught him the harsh realities of life and that men are required to be harsh back in order to claim success.

"Fear from your subordinates should rival that of your enemies," his uncle had told him so many times that he could hear it clear as a summer day in his mind.

Suddenly, the pair of double doors leading into the wide-open living room of his house slammed open. A commanding guy in a black suit walked through.

"Dante, there's been an incident," he said.

The gang leader took another swig, then wiped his mouth with the towel.

"What kind of incident, Kemar?"

Kemar stopped and turned back toward the door he'd entered from. Two guys walked through behind him. They were holding the beaten Flynn under his shoulders and sliding him along the marble floor. They sat him on a wooden chair facing the ring. He groaned in pain and adjusted his legs.

"Flynn was found like this at the gym," Kemar said. "Everyone else was either dead or unconscious."

Dante looked up, his nostrils flaring.

"How many dead?" he asked.

"Two. And two more were taken to the hospital. They all took a hell of a beating. Even Old Man Mauricio."

Dante cursed in frustration, tossed his towel to the floor and stormed to the side of the ring.

"I'm getting sick and tired of the Traidores' petty actions," Dante said, referring to the eastern half of the broken crime syndicate. "It's time to teach them a lesson."

"It wasn't the Traidores," Flynn said, opening his mouth for the first time. "It was someone else."

"Someone?" Dante said, raising his eyebrows. "One guy took on all four of you?"

"There was another at the end." He adjusted the ice pack. "A woman."

Dante nodded sarcastically and climbed out of the ring. He towered over Flynn, who was battered and hunched over in the chair.

"Let me get this straight," Dante said. "The five of you were taken down by a mysterious man and woman?"

"That's not all," Kemar cut in. "We also lost two of our guys earlier this afternoon. It was a car accident, but we believe it was also caused by these two."

Dante snarled.

"Who are they and what the hell do they want?"

Flynn coughed. His jaw still hurt like hell from the blow he'd taken across the face, and though he'd been injected with morphine, his shot-up and broken legs still hurt as well.

"They're Americans," Flynn said. "The woman was on the boat when we took that girl off the coast of Florida. They want her back."

Dante sighed and looked away. He cracked his neck, shook his head, then looked over at Kemar.

"You told me you had this under control, Kemar. You said you'd handle it after the initial issues with the grab in Florida."

The big, intimidating man didn't hesitate or flinch. He'd been friends with Dante since they were kids. They'd risen through the gang ranks together. Had fought side by side for years. He didn't fear his leader nearly as much as the others. But he had a profound level of love and respect for him.

"I underestimated them, Dante," he said. "This guy, Logan Dodge, he's apparently former special forces. And he's a bit of a local hero. Gets into scrapes and comes out on top on a routine basis. And his wife's just as dangerous."

"I don't give a fuck who they are," Dante snapped. "You will track them down and kill them. Pease tell me that you've got something to go on here."

"We have a tail on them and were formulating a strike," Kemar replied. "But I'm not convinced this tactic is best."

"If you have something to say, I suggest you say it."

"He's just after the one girl," Kemar said. "Maybe we should just give her to them."

"Excuse me?" Dante said, stepping toward the much taller guy and staring him in the eye.

"Might be what's best for business. Look what they've done. Four of our guys are dead already. Two more were beaten so badly they'll be out for months. I know she's already been paid for. It looks bad for us to back out, but these things are to be expected in this line of work. There are no guarantees."

Just as the words left Kemar's lips, Dante closed in and grabbed his left wrist as fast as a striking cobra. He slid behind the big guy and pulled his arm back behind him.

"One more word like that, and you and I'll step into this ring with no gloves and no taps, understand?"

Kemar winced as Dante forced his arm into an unnatural and incredibly painful position.

"We do not give in to anyone's demands," Dante declared. "You will rush her processing. Whatever you gotta do, but I want her out of the ranch and ready for delivery as soon as possible. Do you understand?"

Kemar nodded. It was an unheard-of demand. Girls usually spent at least a week at the Ranch before they were ready. Scarlett had only been there for a few hours.

"Yes, Dante. I understand."

Dante pulled harder, just to make sure his message had struck home, then released his second-in-command.

Kemar rolled his shoulder a few times, stretching

it out to relieve the pain.

"And the Americans?" he said as Dante stepped away.

"We still have a tail on them?"

Kemar nodded.

"Kill them in their sleep."

TWENTY-SIX

Ange and I entered our hotel room, locked the door behind us, and did a quick scan of the room before plopping down on the couch. We opened the laptop and went to work researching the Gold N Ivory tobacco farm while taking intermittent glances out the front windows to make sure that our tail was still there. His car was still pulled over and we could barely see his outline through the windshield.

We'd followed many targets in our lives and been followed ourselves more times than we could remember. This guy was standing by. Keeping an eye on us and waiting for the order to make a move. My guess was that he'd get the order once nightfall came. Engaging an unknown enemy can be risky, and minimizing that risk is key. They'd most likely try and attack while we slept.

While learning about the farm, I shot a message to Scott and Deputy Director Wilson, giving them the status and asking for any info they could provide.

We discovered that the farm was located west of Havana in the Pinar del Río province, just a few miles outside the town of Vinales. It was a rural province, known for farming and processing the best tobacco in the world. A nature lover's paradise, and much more laid-back and rustic than the big Cuban cities.

We brought up satellite imagery of the farm. Zooming out, we saw massive fields with rows of green tobacco plants. Structures, trees, and steep mountains also dotted the beautiful landscape. The farm was situated with most of the structures on the western side, right at the base of the mountains. A dirt road cut through the greenery and led to what looked like the only entrance on the northern side.

We checked the GPS and saw that we were about two and a half hours away from the location. It was already after 1900, which meant that it would be dark by the time we got there even if we left right away.

My phone vibrated. I grabbed it and answered the call. Scott and Wilson both answered. They had us on a conference call on a secure line.

"This guy Dante Salazar is bad news," Scott said after a quick greeting. "Heads that gang whose leader we brought down a few summers back."

"I got that much from a cab driver," I said. "The reason he's not behind bars?"

"Big money buys big favors. You know that story well."

"Rap sheet?"

"Just a few charges," Wilson said. "Assault. Drug trafficking. None of them stuck. Oh, and get this: we ran a check on his business partners. Turns out his tobacco farms work closely with the Wake Corporation."

The mention of the name caused my blood to boil.

Richard Wake had been the puppet master behind Carson Richmond and her oil rig corruption back in April of 2009. He was one of the most wealthy and powerful men alive. He also had a knack for being involved in scandals around the world, and for somehow wriggling free of them. He owned many major companies, including one of the world's largest fleets of commercial cargo ships.

"Richard Wake's involved in this?"

"It appears so," Scott said. "All the more reason to always watch your back. You two run into any trouble today?"

Ange and I glanced at each other.

"Nothing major. A few unfriendly confrontations. That's how we were able to learn about the farm and Salazar."

I chose not to mention the car chase, the gym fight, and the fact that I'd been struck by a shotgun pellet.

"Nothing major, huh?" Scott said, his voice dripping with disbelief.

"You guys dig up anything else on the farm?" Ange said.

"It's clean," Wilson said.

"Nothing owned by Salazar can be that clean," I said.

There was a short pause in the line.

"Look, Logan," Scott said. "There's a police task force in Cuba that we think you should get into contact with. They specialize in sex trafficking prevention. If you two are thinking about heading west and taking a closer look at this farm, I suggest you do so with their help."

Neither of us wanted help. We didn't know who we could trust, how deep this rabbit hole went. If we told the wrong person what we were up to, we could be led into a trap and killed. Both of us dead and Scarlett taken away into slavery forever. An outcome that was unacceptable.

"We'll call you later for their contact info," I said finally.

"Don't lie to me."

"Scott, there isn't enough time!" Ange exclaimed.

"Dammit, you two," he said. "You can't do everything on your own. You need backup and we can't provide it. You understand? If you go snooping around major gang-owned compounds, there won't be anyone to call if shit hits the fan. Or I should say, when it hits the fan."

We were going to do a lot more than just snoop. Call it reckless or anything else you wanted to call it. We were going to find Scarlett, and we were going to bring her back.

"Logan," Wilson said in a calm voice once the tension settled, "I can personally vouch for this task force. I'm sending you the number of a woman who's been fighting sex trafficking all over Cuba for years. She's based out of Havana. Her name's Consuelo Sanchez." He paused a moment, sighed. "Look, I know it's hard to know who to trust. But just know that I'd put my life in Sanchez's hands any day of the week and twice on Sunday."

We fell silent. Ange and I glanced at each other. Maybe they were right. Maybe it was pure hubris to try and do everything on our own. I knew Wilson well enough to know that he didn't throw around his trust lightly. He couldn't afford to, given his position.

"Alright," Ange said, answering for us. "Send over her number. We'll give her a call."

"Will do," Wilson said.

"You guys have anything else?" I said.

As always, Scott reminded us to be careful, then we ended the call. I didn't like fighting with one of my oldest and most trusted friends, but he didn't know how attached we'd grown to the girl, even in just the few short days we'd known her.

"Richard Wake," Ange said, shaking her head.

First the gang leader nephew of Benito Salazar, and now Richard Wake? Two of my biggest former adversaries. Things were just getting better and better.

Ange glanced out the window beside us, then rose to her feet for a better look.

"There's more now," she said, motioning down the street.

I rose and peered through the break in the white curtains as well. In addition to the black Chevy, there was a white van pulled over right behind it. I glanced at my watch. With it nearing 2000 and the sun beginning to set, it was time to move on. We needed a vehicle, and we needed to get our butts to the farm.

We packed up our stuff, peeked out through the door, then headed for the stairwell. Keeping a sharp eye out for anyone suspicious, we kept our heads on swivels as we headed upstairs. We barged through a door at the top and came out onto the roof. It was empty. There were a few lines of clothes swaying in the wind and a few scattered plastic chairs. But there was no movement.

Moving toward the back, we vaulted the narrow gap to the adjoining building, then climbed down the fire escape and hopped into a taxi.

"Mario's Four by Fours," I said.

TWENTY-SEVEN

I glanced back through the rear window just to make sure they weren't following us. After two turns and a long straightaway through the downtown traffic, I relaxed a little. No sign of the black Chevy or the van.

Much like our home of Key West, the city seemed to come more alive the darker it got. They were also prepping for the festival that our first cab driver had mentioned. It sounded fun, but unfortunately we had other plans.

He dropped us off at the rental place a few miles south of the hotel. As much as we'd appreciated the convenience and the knowledge we'd gained from taking taxis, it was time for us to get our own set of wheels. And if we were going to be driving to a rural region during the rainy season, I wanted something that could easily handle off-road conditions. Especially given the incident earlier that day.

We picked out a black Jeep Wrangler hardtop with

a four-inch lift, off-road tires, a snorkel, and a winch. Not wanting to have to give the guy our credit card information, I handed him five hundred Cuban Convertible Pesos, which is equivalent to US dollars.

"*El depósito?*" he said.

"*Sí,*" I replied.

He thought for a moment, so I set five hundred more on the table to help him make up his mind.

"*Gracias, señor.*"

He handed me the keys. Just as we hopped into the Jeep, a few lone raindrops splattered against the windshield. By the time I had it started and drove us onto the cross street, it was pouring in thick sheets. Fortunately, I was used to the tropical climate. One second it's dry, the next you better get underneath something or you're gonna be soaked.

We put our destination back into the GPS and headed out of the city. Traffic wasn't as bad as I'd expected, and once we got beyond Havana it was full speed down a three-lane highway.

Half an hour into the trip, the rains finally died off. But the damage had been done. A layer of water covered the roads, puddles filled the ditches, and roadside ponds crept up the banks.

The sun sank far in the distance behind a shroud of clouds. I took in the countryside by the remaining light. The landscape was a drastic shift from Havana. Most of the countryside was flat green-and-brown farmland. Aside from the occasional city we passed through, it felt like a trip even further back in time. I assumed that many of the farmers we spotted were doing the same work that their families had done on that land for generations.

I didn't know a lot about Cuba's history, but I did know that just a few years following Columbus's arrival in 1492, nearly the entire native population of Cuba had been wiped out by a combination of disease and confrontations with the Spanish. Wanting to utilize the rich soil and incredible climate, Spain shipped African slaves to work the sugar plantations. It wasn't until the Spanish-American War of 1898 that Cubans had retaken control of their land and lowered all Spanish flags for good.

The modern-day citizens of Cuba were the sons and daughters of some of the most ardent and passionate revolutionists to ever walk the earth, born into a nation built on struggle and ever-optimistic ideals, despite gloomy circumstances. It was a past to be proud of. But every society has its stains, every respectable group its exceptions. We were on our way to confront and rectify such an exception.

After another half hour passed, and the sky turned dark, I slipped my phone from my pocket.

"I think it's time we gave this Consuelo Sanchez a call," I said.

"Is Logan Dodge about to ask for help?" Ange said with a smile. "What's next? Key West freezing over?"

I chuckled. "Get your camera ready."

I dialed the number Wilson sent me, pressed call, then put it on speakerphone

"This is Sanchez," a strong female voice said just moments after the first ring.

"Officer Sanchez, my name is Logan Dodge. CIA Deputy Director Wi—"

"He told me to be expecting your call," she cut me off. "He said you and your wife snuck into Cuba earlier today to track down a stolen girl. I'm guessing I have you to blame for the high-speed chase and the dead guys at the gym earlier today." She paused a

192

moment, then added, "Really, I don't know whether I should thank you or arrest you."

"You gotta do what you gotta do, Sanchez."

"Oh, great. How refreshing. A cocky American."

"I got no time for banter. I was told that you lead a police task force that fights sex trafficking."

"Go on."

"We have reason to believe that Dante Salazar is using a tobacco farm near Vinales to hide abducted women."

"What farm?"

"One that was formerly owned by his uncle, Benito Salazar. It's called Gold N Ivory."

Sanchez paused a moment.

"What evidence do you have of this?"

"Nothing hard yet. But we'll have it by later tonight if our suspicions are correct."

"Later tonight? What the hell are you talking about?"

I changed lanes to avoid a guy on the side of the road. He was walking beside a donkey that was pulling a wooden cart.

"We're going to pay this farm a visit. Give ourselves a private tour."

She gave a cold laugh. "Sounds like you two are all set to take on the whole gang single-handedly. What did you call me for, then?"

Ange and I exchanged glances. She was as hardheaded as people get.

"Because we need your help," I said. "Not with the sneaking in part. We got that covered. But I'm guessing that once we're inside, there'll be a handful of girls needing help. That's where you come in."

"So, let me get this straight. You two sneak into the farm. Then I show up with a handful of officers

193

once you've done your thing? Do you have any idea how much trouble I could get in for letting you do this? You're in our country illegally."

"Then don't help us," Ange snapped. "No one's forcing your hand here. We called you as a courtesy, not to ask permission. We're here to get a girl back who was taken from us, and we won't stop until we have her or we're dead."

A short silence followed Ange's words. I admired her more than I could describe. She was tough as nails when she needed to be. Didn't take crap from anyone. Never backed down.

"You two are out of your minds," Sanchez finally said. I was about to hang up when she added, "But I can't help but admire your courage and resolve." She sighed. "Where are you now?"

"Little over an hour from the farm," I said.

"Okay. I'll assemble my team as well as a few ambulances and start heading that way. Keep me updated on what happens once you're inside."

She paused a moment, then told us to proceed with caution. She explained how Benito had owned a handful of properties in the western region of Cuba. Farms, houses, and various other scattered properties. All of which had fallen to his nephew Dante upon his death. She told us that he'd most likely have backup nearby in case something went wrong at the farm.

"We'll be cautious," I said.

She paused again, then said, "I want you both to know that the only reason I'm doing this is because the CIA deputy director holds you in such high esteem. We go way back, Wilson and I. If it weren't for his vouching, I'd place a call out for your arrests as soon as we hang up."

"And if it weren't for his recommendation, we

wouldn't have called you in the first place," I said. "Over and out."

We ended the call and I slid my phone back into my pocket.

"I like her," Ange said.

TWENTY-EIGHT

"Five miles out," Ange said. She had the GPS up and glanced intermittently between it and the road ahead of us.

The sun had already set. By the light of the moon, I caught glimpses of the mountains we'd seen while researching back at the hotel. We'd read that they're called mogotes, and that they're giant karst formations, some extending over 1300 feet into the air. They tower over the fields and scattered farmhouses like soldiers on watch.

I followed Ange's instructions, and it wasn't long before we found ourselves on a dirt road. More mud than dirt, given the recent rain. But it was flat, with fresh sets of tire tracks heading in both directions.

Then we turned onto another dirt road. It was narrower. Had fewer tracks.

We soon reached a large wooden sign. It was dark and the sign wasn't lit, but I instantly recognized the name and the gold-and-white color scheme.

I drove past the entrance, and both Ange and I surveyed everything we could see. It wasn't much. The border was lined with tall, widespread trees. The gaps were filled in by a wooden fence that had to be at least eight feet tall. All we could see were small glimpses of the distant roofs of structures.

I'd planned to stop a few hundred yards from the entrance and hop out for a better look, but Ange told me to keep my foot on the gas.

"There's a sentry," she said. She'd crawled in the backseat and was peering through the left side window behind me. "Scratch that. There are two sentries." She moved back into the passenger seat and added, "And they've both got rifles."

"Two highly armed guards at the entrance?" I said. "Seems a little excessive for a tobacco farm, don't you think?" I looked through my open window. "And these tall trees and the fence. None of the other farms we saw on the way here had them."

We continued for half a mile, then reached the edge of the farm. Not seeing anyone around, I pulled over and put the Jeep in park.

"What do you think?" I said. "Hide the car and climb over the walls for some recon?"

Ange paused a moment, then leaned over the dashboard. She looked across the road, across the edge of the farm, up toward the pillar-shaped mountains that were quickly becoming solid black silhouettes.

"Maybe we don't have to jump the fence yet," she said. She motioned toward a tiny dirt road that cut to the left just beyond the corner of the farm. "I'm sure we'd have a nice view from up there with the night vision scope. I mean, we do have a winch."

She had a decent point. It couldn't hurt to try, so long as we didn't draw attention to ourselves.

I shifted back to drive, then hit the gas and cut a left down a narrow dirt path. I doubted it had been used by anything more than horses for years. It was slow going, and we splashed our way through more than one deep pool of muddy water before reaching the base of the nearest mountain. I stopped at the base of it, then looked up. We were just a stone's throw away from the farm's border. Ange was right—from up there we'd have a clear view of the entire place.

I hit the gas, following what looked like it could be a path that cut along the edge of the mountain. I made it halfway up the slippery, muddy slope before having to hop out, grab the winch, then climb my way up and secure it around a wide tree trunk.

I powered it on and rumbled us up the steep and slippery side of the mountain. When we reached the top, I found a cleared flat spot to park the Jeep and killed the engine. I grabbed my backpack, then we hopped out and headed for the edge for a better view. After a few minutes, we found a good spot on a large rock and took in the scene below.

It was a good thing we'd decided on higher ground. The trees and fence completely enclosed the entire farm. Impressive considering I estimated it to be around a thousand acres, or about the size of Central Park.

Most of the farm was dark, the rows of green leaves reflecting the glimpses of moonlight through the occasional breaks in the clouds. Off to the east, there were pens filled with horses and various livestock. There were also rows of small huts and sheds with carts and various farming equipment.

Only a few lights glowed in the darkness, and they

were near the farmhouses. I grabbed my night vision monocular from my backpack and powered it on. Focusing through the lens, I scanned every inch of the structures and spotted three more guys with guns. Two of them were standing beside the front of the largest structure, and the third was patrolling around the back of it.

After a few minutes, I handed the monocular to Ange. "That farmhouse is the most heavily guarded," I said.

She held it up to her right eye and scanned the scene below us. After looking over the farmhouse, she directed her gaze down along the southwestern edge of the farm.

"There's a creek with trees and thick bushes along its shores," she said. "It runs along the backside of the farm. Travels right beside the back of the farmhouse." She paused a moment, then nodded. "Looks like our best bet."

Suddenly, the distant groan of a big diesel engine tore through the still night air. It was coming from the main dirt road that ran along the front of the farm. We looked toward the sound and saw the bright headlights of a truck as it pulled into the entrance. We were far off, but the zoom of the scope allowed Ange to see the interaction at the gate.

"Looks like the sentries know the driver," she said. "They just waved them in."

The large gate opened and the truck rumbled through. It motored on the dirt road that cut straight through the heart of the farm and slowed in front of the largest farmhouse. The two guys who'd been standing idly by pushed open the large doors, and the truck disappeared from view.

I rose from my kneeling position and stretched.

"I've seen enough," I said. "From what we've read, this is a very peaceful province. I see no reason for the walls or the armed guards if it's a normal farm." I glanced back at the Jeep, then added, "You get set up with your sniper up here and cover me. I'm going in."

"Yeah, right." She lowered the monocular and rose to her feet beside me. "Twice today you've gone in without me. The second time you nearly ended up looking like a piñata at the end of a party. We're going in together this time, and that's final."

TWENTY-NINE

We parked the Jeep along the base of the mountain where it was concealed from view by thick trees. Then we donned our bulletproof vests and trekked the quarter of a mile around to the southwest corner of the farm. It was quiet and dark, and we saw no movement as we climbed up into a baobab tree and stepped out onto one of its thick branches.

The top of the fence had loops of razor wire, so we brought one of the Jeep's floor mats and draped it over to prevent getting sliced to pieces. Some ideas are the product of training, some personal experience. I had Tyler Durden from *Fight Club* to thank for that one.

We landed softly inside the farm. Keeping to the shadows, we moved toward the creek and used the trees to cover our approach to the big farmhouse.

When we were within a few hundred yards, we stopped and took another look around. What I've found in my years of experience infiltrating enemy compounds, is that patience and surprise are key. We wanted to be as sure as we could of what we were getting ourselves into before we made our move. And we wanted to keep our presence a secret for as long as possible.

We scanned the back of the farmhouse. The patrolling sentry was still walking back and forth and looked bored out of his mind. He wore fatigues and had good posture and a clean rifle. He looked up at the stars, then down at his feet, humming a song to himself. It was vaguely familiar but didn't ring any distinct bells. Benny Moré, perhaps.

We watched as he turned to show his back to us, then walked to a slow rhythm in the direction he'd come. When he was halfway down the back side of the farmhouse, we made our move.

Quickly, quietly, and after taking one more look around to make sure nobody else had approached, we took off for the side of the structure. Once clear of the corner, we dropped down and waited for the guy to return. He did so slowly. Part of me wanted to just sprint over and take him down, but we wanted to be as quiet as possible. We didn't know how many guys were on site or nearby waiting to be called in as backup, but I estimated that the number was high.

The sentry came within one step of the edge when his radio crackled to life.

"*Actualización de estado?*" a voice said through the speaker, asking for a status update.

"*Callado como una tumba*," the sentry replied.

Quieter than a grave.

The man clipped the radio back onto his belt. We couldn't have asked for better timing. We'd have at least ten minutes before anyone was likely to call in

202

for another update, probably more like thirty.

When the guy took one more step, Ange sprang around the corner and pounced on him. She placed a hand around his mouth to keep him quiet, then wrapped an arm around his neck and brought him steadily to the ground. He kicked and groaned and struggled, then went motionless.

"Nicely done, Fox," I said, calling her by her maiden name.

We dragged his body into the shadows, grabbed his radio, and hid him under a pile of discarded leaves. After taking one more look around, we moved along the corner and straight for the small back door of the farmhouse. We both grabbed hold of our handguns, unsure of what we were going to encounter when we barged in and said hello.

On a silent count of three, I pushed open the door and we both swarmed in. My eyes scanned over every inch of the massive space, the sights of my Sig following every move. We took a few steps, and within seconds we had the whole place covered. Most of the space was filled nearly floor to ceiling with stacks of dried tobacco leaves. The truck was parked beside the massive doors, but there was nobody in or near it. No movement of any kind.

The smell was powerful, but actually pretty good. More sweet than anything else. Aside from the voices of the two guys talking just outside, it was perfectly silent.

We moved to the center of the room. When we got there, we looked at each other confused.

There were no partitions. It was just one big space, with two visible points of entry or exit.

So where is the driver? And what is he hauling into the barn at this time of night?

I peeked into the cab of the truck. Completely empty. I moved around to the back and pushed aside the canvas. Empty as well. The bed was dirty and contained a few old stray leaves and nothing more.

I listened to the muffled conversation just outside the door, and my head naturally dropped down. It was then that I saw it. Tracks on the floorboards. A cluster of fresh muddy boot prints that led around the left side of the truck. Keeping my head down, I followed them.

They didn't lead to the half-empty stacks of bags of processed tobacco. Instead, they led to an open space in the floor with a wooden cart. There they ended. Just vanishing into thin air. I knelt down and examined them. It was dark, but my natural night vision had adjusted. None of the tracks headed back toward the truck.

"Ange, check this out," I said as I stepped toward the cart.

She strode over from the far side of the room.

I grabbed the edges of the cart. They were in serious need of some WD-40, but I managed to force the reluctant wheels to turn and pushed the cart aside.

"A trap door?" she said.

She arrived just as the cart rolled away, revealing a square cut in the floorboards. One of the sides was covered in dents and scratches. I dropped down, pressed my fingers into the edges, and pulled up. The floor came loose, then swung skyward on a hinge. The secret passageway was nearly pitch black, but the light bleeding in from the outside lights allowed me to see deviations.

"There's a staircase," Ange said, leaning over my shoulder. "Now why would an ordinary tobacco farm need a secret hatch and an underground passageway?"

I grabbed my flashlight from the backpack and switched it on at low power. The wooden stairs dropped down into the earth, then the path disappeared under the edge of the opening.

I glanced up at Ange. I'd tell her "ladies first," but she'd hop right in. Regardless of her experience and ability to hold her own, if someone was going to fall into a trap, I wanted it to be me.

Keeping the light shining, I dropped down onto the creaky steps. Ange was right on my heels and we moved down the steps and onto a dirt base. After a few minutes of playing Indiana Jones, the dirt-and-wood-framed passageway shifted to solid rock. The space widened dramatically and the air became noticeably cooler.

We'd entered a cave.

"You'd mentioned earlier at the hotel that this province was known for large cave systems," I said.

"Some of the largest and most beautiful in the Caribbean. Or so I read. The caves were apparently created by underground rivers through the mogotes."

We followed the cavern for a minute before it opened up. The top extended up to over forty feet and was covered with stalactites that reached down to corresponding stalagmites below. It reminded me of Luray Caverns in Virginia, and more recently, the caves Scott and I had explored in Sierra Gorda, Mexico, while tracking down the Aztec treasure. Had we been there under different circumstances, I would have spent some time appreciating it.

"Wait a second," Ange whispered, raising a hand. "I hear something."

We both paused and listened. Sounds were coming from deeper in the cave. Muffled voices that reverberated off the cool, smooth rock face. And what sounded like a woman crying.

Ange and I glanced at each other, raised our handguns, and moved in. We'd been tracking down Scarlett, putting our necks on the line to find her all day, and we were finally closing in on her.

I switched my flashlight to the lowest setting and watched my step as we moved in the direction of the sounds. Soon they became distinct. It was three men talking. The crying had quieted to a whimper, but it was clear that the girl making the sound was close by.

We moved into a sharp turn. I quickly switched off the light as a well-lit chamber came into view. The three guys we heard were sitting at a table playing poker. Along the far wall of the chamber, there were rows of openings in the rock. Small spaces with metal bars. They were each very dark inside, but I could see the outline of a seated woman in one of them, her long dark hair covering her face.

Loud screams echoed from an adjoining room. A man wearing a white lab coat stepped into the chamber. He was carrying a metal briefcase in one hand and a syringe in the other.

The girl's sounds from the other room grew louder. I heard punches being thrown, a man cursing, and the woman struggling.

This was it. The Ranch. The place where they brought kidnapped women to be "processed."

I felt a deep sickening feeling in my gut. Few things ticked me off more than sex trafficking, and we'd stumbled into the well-organized and evil heart of a large-scale operation. I wasn't sure how many girls were there, but there were over twenty cells in that chamber alone. For all we knew there were a handful more chambers just like it.

There was no explaining or justifying what we were seeing. These guys were all stone-cold killers, soulless gangsters making their living at the expense of the moral fiber that makes us human. They'd made their decision, and it was time for us to make ours.

No more recon, no more exploration. This is strike hard with everything you've got time.

I looked over the three guys drinking and playing cards. One had an AK-47 hanging over the back of his seat by its sling. The other two each had handguns on the table in front of them. Those two would be our first targets. Their weapons would be much easier to grab and aim than a rifle would be.

"I got revolver on the right," Ange said, reading my mind.

We both raised our weapons.

Here we go.

"Three…," I whispered. "two… one."

We popped around the corner, took aim, and fired. The loud cracks of gunpowder thundered in the confines of the cave. Near-perfect synchronization. Near-perfect shots. Both center mass. The unsuspecting card players jerked sideways. Blood splattered against the cavern wall behind them, and they fell to the ground.

The third guy freaked out and spun around. He knocked his beer over, spilling the liquid onto the table. Before he could grab his AK, Ange and I both took him down. Two 9mm rounds tore through his chest. He flailed back lifelessly, slammed onto the table, then fell to the ground beside his dead poker buddies.

Ange and I stormed into the chamber, both on a mission. The clock was ticking now. Everything with ears in those caves knew that something was going down.

The guy in the white lab coat fell to his knees as we approached. He was paralyzed by fear. Paralyzed by the loud noises, the sight of death, and the sudden danger.

By the time we reached him, he'd summoned just enough courage to make him a target. He dropped the briefcase. Dropped the syringe. But reached for something in his coat pocket. Something metal and pointy.

He lunged toward Ange and tried to skew her with his medical scissors. Before I could pull the trigger on my Sig, she handled the situation.

Sliding back, she grabbed his wrist with her left hand and twisted. More than one bone snapped. He yelled and she pulled him close, slammed her Glock into his forehead to shut him up.

I covered her, keeping a sharp eye on the two other passageways jutting out from the main chamber.

A few girls had taken cover in their cells. A few others were peeking down at the activity. They were all pretty but overcome with despair. I counted six in all.

None of them were Scarlett.

Suddenly, angry yells echoed from down the opposite passageway. Stomping feet followed.

Ange and I took off. The passage dug thirty feet or so into the rock before turning into another chamber. This one was just as big as the first. More cells and large chambers lined one of the walls. It was two stories high with a metal set of stairs.

Two guys with guns ran along the center of the chamber. A third covered them from above as he approached the top of the staircase.

We darted sideways and took aim just as they

came into view. Two more quick shots. Two more down and out. I managed to strike the guy on the right in the neck. Ange caught her mark in the face. Both whipped back and slammed hard onto the ground.

The third guy had a minuscule window of opportunity to make a retaliation. Ange and I dove off in separate directions to avoid his gunfire.

He managed to fire off a slew of sporadic automatic rounds before I took aim and put a bullet through his left thigh. The blow knocked his feet out from under him. His momentum did the rest. He fell forward, his face slamming into the edge of a metal stair with a crack before the rest of his body rolled down to the bottom.

In the calm after the storm, Ange and I fell silent, listening intently for any signs of enemy life. It was silent aside from a few crying girls and the distant sound of rushing water coming from a cave across from us.

We crossed the chamber and scanned over every inch of the place. There were only two ways in or out of that one, and we didn't hear anyone else in either direction. We were in the clear, at least for the time being.

We moved along the cells, one at a time. Two more girls at the bottom. A third up top. Still no sign of Scarlett. While looking over the girls, I stumbled into a large space with folders stacked on tables, and pictures and maps all over the walls.

Holy shit.

It was an intel room. A treasure trove of vital information. It was intel that, if utilized properly, could be used to put an end to their entire operation.

Ange stepped in behind me and we started taking pictures. I focused in on a map that appeared to show the traffickers' movements throughout the western part of the country. It showed lines from Havana to where we were at the farm. A different-colored line was drawn from the farm to a spot along the coast near a town called Santa Lucia.

I froze when I saw pictures and names of police officers. A few were circled in red, most were crossed out. A few of the names had lines connecting them to Sanchez's countertrafficking task force, with her picture at the top. I took a quick snap of the top of the hierarchy. Not only was this Sanchez woman trusted by Wilson, but it looked like she was also on the gang's watch list. A good sign.

After taking a handful of pictures, I stepped back out into the chamber then headed up the cave toward the entrance until I got a signal on my sat phone. Once there, I looked around then called Sanchez. It was a quick conversation. We didn't have any time to waste. I told her where we were, that we'd taken down a handful of gang members and that we had a group of scared girls who needed help and pickup right away.

She and a team were already on their way. As I'd expected, they'd left Havana right after our conversation earlier. They were on the road, roughly twenty minutes out from the farm.

I ended the call and stepped back down into the main chamber. I returned just as Ange found a large two-pole knife switch and slid it to the on position. A loud mechanical groan filled the air, then all of the cell doors screeched open in unison.

"Sanchez's twenty minutes out," I said.

She nodded and we went through each holding cell one at a time. We cared for each of the women as best we could. Most of them were so delirious that they didn't know what was happening. They were scared and dirty. The smell of the cells was rank.

As fast as we could, we ushered them to the first chamber and gathered them up with the rest. I was amazed at how easily they responded to orders. It was like they were brain-dead. I glanced down at the broken syringe beside the guy in the lab coat and wondered at the type and amount of drugs they'd put into each girl to make them so submissive and calm.

"You're all safe now," Ange said, addressing the group. If they were listening or had any understanding of what was happening, their body language didn't show it. "We're going to get you all out of here. But first, we need your help."

I pulled my phone out of my pocket and brought up my pictures.

"Have you seen this girl?" I held up the screen, which displayed the picture I'd taken of Ange and Scarlett on the swim platform of the Baia before her first time scuba diving.

I zoomed in and pointed at Scarlett's face.

We showed each of the girls the picture, one at a time. A few were too out of it to even respond. The ones who did said only one painful word. No.

No. No. No.

We were running out of time. Ange and I both knew that at any moment, an army of backup could arrive and engage us.

But when I held the screen in front of the second to-last-girl, a very young-looking black girl with bright blue eyes, she hesitated.

"Mi si har todeh," the girl said in a Jamaican accent. "Shi here very short time. Less dan one day mi tink. Days run togeddah here. Many girls come an guh."

"Where is she?" Ange said. "What happened to her?"

The girl swallowed.

"Dem tek har away. Dat way." She pointed across the cavern, toward the cave that split off toward the sounds of rushing water.

"How long ago?" I said, kneeling down beside her and staring into her eyes. "When did they take her away?"

"Nuh lang. Maybe a hour."

"Ange, stay here," I said, rising to my feet. "Yell out if anyone comes. I won't go far."

I took off across the cavern, through the passageway and the adjoining cavern. I grabbed my flashlight and switched it on. The narrow cut zigzagged a few times, and the flowing water sounds grew louder and louder.

Moving deeper, I came upon a strong wrought-iron gate. It was secured by a thick-linked chain and a big lock.

Looking past the metal bars, I spotted a waterfall. It cascaded to a deep murky channel below. I could just barely make out what looked like a small dock.

Holy shit. An underground river. That's how these guys are transporting the girls out of here.

I pictured it in my mind. Girls taken from all over. Transported to Cuba via cargo ships. Conditioned at this hellhole. Then transported via boat back to the coast.

I grabbed hold of the bars and shook the gate with all my strength. It barely budged. The chain was strong, the lock high quality. It would take a hell of a lot more than a few well-placed rounds to break it. It would take some heavy explosives.

All out of options, I turned and darted back toward

Ange and the girls. I felt a wave of disappointment rush over me. We'd been so close. So close to finding Scarlett and liberating her. Less than an hour close. And we were left in the bowels of a powerful crime syndicate's pride and joy with a group of kidnapped girls. I could practically feel the furious beast breathing down our necks. An angry army of criminals that I had no doubt was at that very moment grabbing their pitchforks and closing in on us.

THIRTY

My heart sank as the sounds of a woman's screams echoed throughout the cave.

I ran as fast as I could toward the sound. It was coming toward the first chamber, where I'd left Ange and the girls.

I sprang around the corner with my Sig raised. Ange was kneeling down beside the wailing woman, trying to comfort her. There was no danger. Nothing aside from the harm that had already been caused. A scar that these women would have for the rest of their lives.

I ran over and knelt down beside them. The girl was talking nonsense to herself. Ange tried to calm her down and snap her out of it, but nothing helped.

"She needs water," one of the girls said. "We all do. The drugs make us dehydrated."

I looked over my shoulder at the girl who'd spoken. Before I could ask, she pointed to a barrel in the corner. I ran over and filled an aluminum bottle, then gave it to Ange, who eased it into the frantic girl's mouth. She spat out most of it, but what did make it down her throat seemed to help.

"Please, help yourselves to it," I said softly to the other women.

They looked at me with wide eyes. For however long it'd been since they were taken, they'd been ordered what to do at all times. It had clearly been a while since they'd been allowed to help themselves to anything.

I ushered a few girls over and broke off the top of the barrel. They used the cups to quench their thirst, then all the other girls joined in. After a minute, I helped Ange and the girl to their feet.

"Scarlett?" Ange said.

"The way is gated and locked. There's an underground river beyond and a dock. I'm sure she's a long ways away by now."

She bit her lip. Her eyes were watery. She wiped a tear, then gasped as she looked down.

"Hey," I said, wrapping an arm around her and holding her close. "It's going to be okay. We're going to find her." I squeezed her tighter. Our eyes met. "We'll find her, Ange."

I held her for half a minute. The whole thing was taking a huge toll on her. Seeing innocent young girls treated that way is enough to make you puke.

She looked back up at me, then we both glanced at the other girls. There were six in all. Neither of us had to say a word. We could read each other's minds. We'd go after Scarlett, yes, but first we were going to get those girls the hell out of there.

I glanced at my watch. It was just after midnight. It had been ten minutes since I'd spoken to Sanchez.

That meant we still had another ten minutes or so before the cavalry arrived.

I glanced at Ange, who was reading my mind. We couldn't just sit tight and wait. We had to move, to get out of there and close the gap between us, Sanchez, and her officers.

"We need to get out of here," I said, addressing the group of girls. "We can help you, but you have to do as we say. And you've got to keep quiet. Understand?"

There were a few girls who clearly couldn't understand English, so I repeated everything in Spanish. They nodded softly, and I motioned toward the main passageway into the cave system.

"Okay. Let's move."

I took the lead, Ange the rear. I kept my flashlight aimed forward, providing a beam of light to illuminate my way while Ange shined hers as well. We expected a flood of gang members to come pouring in at any second, so we both had our weapons at the ready.

We soon reached the staircase.

No sign of anyone yet.

I halted the group and listened. The hatch was still shut and there were no sounds coming from inside the tobacco barn. I took the creaky steps slowly, then pushed up the trap door and had a look around. The room was empty. The cart, the stacks of tobacco, the tracks, the truck—everything was just as we'd left it.

I pushed the hatch open all of the way, then motioned for the girls to follow. Making my way slowly across the room, I saw the shadows of the two sentries still standing just outside the large doors. Being so deep in the caves, they apparently hadn't heard the gunshots. And obviously no alarm had been raised.

As quietly as possible, we motioned the girls over to the back of the truck. It was the only way we could all get out of there fast. Use the gangsters' transportation against them.

Naturally, the girls were hesitant to get back into truck that had taken them to that hellhole.

"It's the only way," Ange told them. "We sure aren't all piling into the four-seater that we drove here in."

We helped them up one at a time. The dark-skinned girl who'd told us about Scarlett stopped at the tailgate.

"Yuh wid di police?" she asked.

"No," I replied. "Just a couple of pissed-off civilians."

She coughed and wiped her teary eyes.

"Shh," I said, placing a finger to my mouth. "There are guys on the other side of that door."

I spoke clearly, though in a whisper. The shadows of the two sentries didn't move. They hadn't heard anything, yet. I heard their occasional muffled voices. Shooting the breeze and combating the late-night boredom.

Once the girls were inside and sitting down, we assured them again that we were getting them all out of this. We also told them to hold on, we were undoubtedly in for a very bumpy ride. Then we lifted the tailgate into place and secured the dark green canopy.

Ange and I climbed into the cab. The keys were on the dash.

I gave a quick call to Sanchez. She told me they were just a few minutes from the farm, and I replied that we were heading out to meet her. I told her to keep a lookout for a big truck with a green canopy. Before she could tell me to hang tight and wait for her, I hung up.

The last thing I wanted was to sit there and wait. I didn't know how many more gang members there were on site. For all we knew, there was an entire barracks of armed men just waiting for the word.

"What do you wanna do about them?" Ange whispered, motioning toward the shadows of the two sentries just outside the doors.

She was eyeing them through the side mirrors.

Just as the words left her lips, I heard a loud voice coming from just outside. It was followed by a loud whistle. Right away I knew that the jig was up. Somehow they'd figured out what had happened.

They must've found the sentry we took down.

Instinctively, I grabbed hold of the keys and slid the big one into the ignition. I glanced through my big side mirror. The two shadows outside were moving back and forth; voices were yelling out orders. I knew they were about to move and wanted to catch them before they had the chance.

"Ever read *Mr. Mercedes*?" I said, answering Ange's question with one of my own.

It was time for me to take a page right out of the Stephen King book about a deranged lunatic obsessed with plowing down pedestrians in his Mercedes.

I flicked my wrist. The large diesel engine rumbled to life. I put the truck in reverse and stomped on the gas. The massive tires screeched on the wood floor. We accelerated as fast as the five-ton cargo truck could.

The back frame of the truck shattered through the door, sending debris in all directions. I caught a brief glimpse of the two sentries. Their eyes were massive.

Like deer caught in the headlights. They tried to move, but the back of the truck pummeled into them and the wheels bounced as we drove over their bodies like small speed bumps.

I had one hand on the wheel and the other clutching my Sig. With the window rolled down, I was ready to fire off a few rounds just in case. But as we continued to rumble and pick up backward speed, I saw their motionless bodies lying in the dirt. Broken, battered, and no longer an issue.

I let off the gas and braked us to a skidded stop. Putting the truck in drive, I floored it again and spun the wheel. I put us right in the center of the road, cruising out of the farm. I brought us up to sixty miles an hour as we roared through the dark open landscape. Soon, we heard the faint sound of sirens from far in the distance.

We ran into trouble at the gate. We could see the sentry walking toward us with his rifle against his shoulder.

"Ange!" I said, but she was already on it.

She leaned out the passenger window, took aim, and fired a succession of bullets straight at the lone sentry. Even with us bumping and bouncing, she struck him in the side and he fell just as his finger pressed the trigger. I ducked and two bullets crashed through the windshield and buried themselves in the seat back beside me.

The guy fell. He pressed a hand to his chest and reached for his dropped weapon. Not quick enough. I plowed into him at just over sixty miles per hour. I could hear his bones break from the force of the solid grille, his life taken in an instant.

With the sentry down, I kept my foot on the gas and bashed through the metal gate with a loud crash.

The truck shuddered from the impact and I nearly lost control. I let off the gas and braked as I spun onto the dirt road. I slid the big truck to a stop. A cloud of dust rose up into the headlights.

I hit the gas again but soon slowed to a stop as a wall of police SUVs and ambulances headed straight for us. I pulled over and the blaring lights and sounds closed in on us. Three police cars stopped fifty feet in front of us, the two ambulances right behind.

A Hispanic woman wearing black pants, a white button-up shirt, and a bulletproof vest stepped into view. She held a Makarov 9mm pistol in her right hand as she cautiously approached the driver's-side door.

"Logan Dodge?" she said, eyeing both of us through the windshield.

She had a powerful presence. A commanding voice that was even more impressive than it had been on the phone. There was no mistaking her. She was everything I'd expected and more.

I nodded.

"You sure know how to make an exit," she said. "Out of the truck. Now."

"The girls are in the back," I said as I climbed down, my boots squishing onto the muddy road.

"Any more gang members nearby?"

"Not that I know of. But there's at least eight dead in the compound. A few unconscious."

She turned to face the other officers and waved them over.

"Get the paramedics over here," she yelled.

We moved toward the back. Opened up the canvas. Dropped down the tailgate. Sanchez shined her flashlight into the group of twelve scared faces staring back at us.

The paramedics ran over and climbed up into the truck. One by one they examined the women. Some were in worse shape than others. They picked five from the group and we helped them down to the road.

"I want all of them taken to the hospital," one of the paramedics said. He was a middle-aged man with glasses and an authoritative tone. "They all need to be checked. We'll take these five in the ambulances."

Sanchez nodded.

"We'll take them in squad cars." She looked up at the remaining girls and motioned for them to come down. "Alright, let's go. You're all safe now. Nobody's gonna hurt you anymore."

The three of us stepped away as a handful of officers flooded over to help the girls down.

"Any more in the farm?" Sanchez asked.

"Not that we saw. But maybe."

"The cave system is extensive," Ange chimed in.

After a moment, I glanced at my watch. We were losing time, and we hadn't had much to work with in the first place.

"We'd love to stay and chat, but we need to get moving," I said. "We got a vehicle parked about a mile and a half from here. We could use a ride."

"Where are you going?"

"Santa Lucía," Ange said. "There's a private dock there that was marked as part of the gang's network."

"They could very well already be gone," she said. "I have a contact in the Havana underworld who's informed me that Salazar's chopper just took off from his house in Havana. Heading west. By the time you reach Santa Lucía, it could be too late."

"Or we could be just in time to take him down," Ange snapped. "Either way, we're going. And if you could give us a lift to our Jeep, it would be greatly appreciated. If not, then quit stalling and just tell us. I could use a good run anyway."

She stared back at Ange. Felt the fire burning within her.

"Wilson told me you two were the most determined people he'd ever met," she said. "I hadn't believed him at first." She turned and motioned for us to follow her. "Come on. I'll have someone drive you to your Jeep."

One of Sanchez's subordinates drove us over to where we'd parked the Jeep and dropped us off. We sprinted for the doors and jumped inside. I started up the V-6 engine, put it in gear, and hit the gas. It was just under an hour to Santa Lucía. An hour that we didn't have.

I thundered the Jeep full speed. It tackled the bumpy dirt road with ease. I'd always felt that Jeeps drove better off-road. It's their bread and butter, and boy do they savor it.

Once we were on the highway, I pulled out my sat phone and punched in Jack's number.

THIRTY-ONE

Jack Rubio sat at the stern of the trawler. He sang along to Jimmy Buffett's "Son of a Son of a Sailor" while leaning back and watching the two poles with their lines paid out. The engines were running on cruise control. Ten knots.

After dropping off Logan and Angelina earlier that day, he'd sweet-talked his way past the Cuban Coast Guard and headed out to the open waters of the straits. He'd told Logan he'd stand by in case they needed a lift back home. With nothing else to do, he rigged a few poles and had been trolling along for a few scattered hours throughout the day.

Atticus lay on the deck beside him. He was tired after a long day of playing fetch in the water. His eyes closed occasionally, then popped open when Jack would join Jimmy in a high note.

Just as he was belting out the end to one of his favorite verses, his phone interrupted him. He slid off the chair, turned down the music, and grabbed it from the bench.

"Yellow?" he said.

"Jack?" a strong male voice said through the speaker. "Are you drunk?"

Atticus jumped to his feet and wagged his tail.

"Logan? Damn, it's good to hear your voice, bro," he said. "Ange there?"

"I'm here, Jack. You doing alright by yourself?" Ange's voice came over the speaker.

"I'm not alone. I got Atty to keep me company. Plus a few marlins."

He quickly explained how he'd been deep sea fishing in international waters all day.

"You find her yet?"

"Getting there, Jack," Logan said. "The snakes keep slipping through our fingers. But we're right on their asses."

"Good. You need me for anything yet?"

"How's the fuel?"

"No problemo. She's still got just over half in the main. Pegged aux and backup. I could do a solid three hundred miles at cruising."

He didn't need to get up and step into the pilothouse to check. He'd looked them over half an hour earlier and knew the burn was minimal at his current speed.

"Good," Logan said, "'cause we're gonna need pickup."

"Just tell me when and where, bro. Though it might be tricky now that I'm on Cuba's radar."

"Head for a spot on a twelve-mile straight northern line from Santa Lucía."

He stepped into the cockpit. He already had a chart of western Cuba out on the table and weighted down with a few full Coke cans and a book. He quickly found Santa Lucía. He was only about thirty miles northeast from where Logan wanted him.

"Twelve miles off Santa Lucía. Alright, I can be there in forty-five minutes."

"Steer clear of the territorial waters. Just stand by there for now. We'll call you. Oh, and keep an eye out for a cargo ship heading out away from the mainland. If you see one, call us right away."

"You got it, bro."

They ended the call, and he set his phone back on the bench. Grabbing his poles one at a time, he quickly and efficiently reeled them in, broke them down, and stowed them in the port compartment.

Petting Atticus, he said, "Alright, boy. Let's go save your parents."

He stepped into the cockpit, where he grabbed hold of a mug and downed what was left of the coffee in it. It was cold, but that didn't matter. He just needed the caffeine boost.

He punched his desired destination into the advanced GPS system. Once it popped up, he eased the throttles forward. The big engines grumbled and the boat accelerated. He swept into a wide banking turn, then brought the trawler up to forty knots, motoring into the darkness.

THIRTY-TWO

I hung up the phone and placed it on the seat between us, glancing at the speedometer. We were flying down the road at just over ninety miles per hour, my heavy foot pushing the vehicle to its limit.

"How far out?" I asked, glancing over at Ange.

"Thirty," she said.

She had her phone in front of her.

I willed the Jeep to go faster. I thought about Scarlett. How we'd managed to just miss her back at the farm. She was scared and mistreated and alone. We needed to get to her before…

My phone vibrated. Ange answered it. She quickly put it on speakerphone.

"Logan, this is Officer Lopez," the rigid voice said. "We've got local officers on scene at the Santa Lucía maritime shipping facility. The place is cleared out. I repeat, no sign of Salazar or his gang members."

I braked, pulled us to a stop along the side of the road.

"Coast Guard on it?" I said, my voice raised. "They could've already left."

"That's a negative. No cargo ships in the nearby offshore area."

Shit.

Ange handed me my phone and I brought up the pictures I'd taken of their transport network. Based on the maps, it was clear that the shipping facility at Santa Lucía was their primary extraction point.

If they aren't getting out from there, then where?

"Salazar's spooked," Ange said. She was staring out through the windshield, lost in thought. "He needs to get out of Cuba as quickly as possible. And he knows it. A ship just won't cut it."

We fell silent for a second.

"He's gonna try and fly out," I said.

Ange nodded.

She scooted beside me and peered at the image of the map. There were a few lines sprouting out from the farm. None led to an airport.

"Sanchez, you still there?" I said.

The line was still live, but she hadn't spoken in a while.

"Roger that," she said. "The closest airport is in Pinar del Río. About fifteen miles in the opposite direction from the farm."

We went quiet again. The opposite direction didn't make sense, and there was no location on the gang's map marking anything near Pinar. But we couldn't help getting the sinking feeling that we were wrong. If we were, we were dead wrong. The plane would take off any minute and we'd never make it in time.

I gazed down at the screen, hoping to spot

something I'd missed. There had to be another option. There had to be something closer that we could close in on.

I thought back to our first conversation with Sanchez earlier that day. When Dante's uncle Benito had come up, she'd mentioned how he'd owned properties all over Cuba. Houses, farms, and seemingly random plots of land.

"Sanchez," I said, "can you give me the location of the other properties that were formerly owned by Benito?"

There was a brief pause.

"I'll need to call you back. Give me a minute."

She hung up without a reply. The seconds seemed to stretch painfully long. Thankfully, it didn't take her a full minute.

"Aside from the tobacco farm and the dock," she said, "he owned two more properties. A cabin near Punta de la Sierra, and hundreds of acres of nothing just east of Minas de Matahambre."

"Can you send me the coordinates for both?"

She did, and we punched them into the GPS. The cabin was located in a mountainous area that was riddled with trees, but the second was perfectly flat. There was nothing to be seen in the endless green fields aside from a large structure and a road to it.

"This spot near Minas de Matahambre looks promising," Ange said.

"There's nothing but rural farmland out that way," Sanchez said. "There sure as hell aren't any airports."

"Not an airport," I said, "but land long and flat enough to take off a plane."

"You're making a lot of speculations here," Sanchez said.

"That's all we've got, Sanchez. Over and out."

I ended the call. Looking over at Ange for affirmation, I got a slight nod.

It was like when a football team's down by a touchdown with ten seconds on the clock and no timeouts. There was no downside to throwing a Hail Mary at that point in the game. If he wasn't there, our final option would be to track down his remaining gang members and force them to tell us where he had run off to. Which was what we'd do if we didn't cruise over to the property.

Just before putting the Jeep back into gear, I heard the faint but unmistakable sound of helicopter rotors. We had the windows rolled down. The sound was growing louder. Ange heard it too. She leaned out the passenger window and peered up into the darkness.

A low-flying chopper roared into view ahead of us. It was a solid black silhouette against the moonlit sky aside from two blinking lights. It flew in from the east and was heading west.

It was on a direct course for the flat, massive property I'd marked as our destination. There was little doubt in my mind whose helicopter it was.

Ange leaned back into the cab and plopped onto her seat.

I hit the gas, kicking up mud as the off-road tires gained traction. We accelerated back onto the main road. GPS said we were ten minutes away. I was going to cut that time in half. I just hoped it would be enough.

THIRTY-THREE

Dante Salazar sat in the cabin of the Mil Mi-8 helicopter. He puffed a cigar to try and relax, but he couldn't sit still. He brushed a strand of his long dark hair from his face and adjusted his headset. He peered out at the dark landscape below, then realized that his hand was shaking.

It wasn't fear that gripped him but anger. Anger and disbelief at the events that had transpired that day. Just before takeoff, he'd received word that the two Americans had infiltrated the Ranch, the tobacco farm that had acted as a base of operations for him and his sex-trafficking ring for years.

Was it hubris on my part? he thought. *Was it foolish not to have heightened the security even more?*

There had been eleven of his soldiers on site during the attack. Eleven armed and experienced gang members.

How in the hell did two fucking people do all of this?

The question puzzled him beyond comprehension. The more he thought about it, the angrier he became. They'd bested him, taken down his operation, and freed an entire batch of profitable women.

No, they haven't bested me yet, he told himself. *This is just a small faction. We will escape, meet up with comrades abroad, and we will grow larger than before.*

After all, he had friends in very high places. Rich and powerful. Elite and with connections.

"We're beginning our descent," the captain said into the headset.

Dante nodded.

"Good," he replied. "I want to be back airborne in under five minutes." He turned to Kemar. "What's the status on our cargo?"

"They will arrive on site any second now," he said. "The plane is in place, fully fueled. The pilots already performed all of their checks." The big guy paused a moment, then added, "I received word from the security guard at the dock in Santa Lucía that police officers are on site and searching the place."

Dante smiled.

They'd taken the bait. And it was a good thing too.

So much had gone wrong in such a short period of time. There was no room for any more mistakes. No more margin for error.

The pilots brought the chopper around and landed it in a field beside a large metal building. By all appearances, the structure looked run-down and abandoned. In reality, it was a secret hangar bay.

Originally conceived and built by his late uncle, the property had been purchased and transformed to

231

act as a last-resort airport in the event that a quick and seamless escape from the country was necessary. Dante had never used it before. But the time had undoubtedly come.

Just as the wheels touched down, Kemar slid open the door and Dante hopped out. He was followed by Kemar and two of his personal bodyguards.

The twin-engine small Soviet aircraft had been moved from the hangar bay and was ready at the edge of the makeshift runway. Two pickup trucks were parked just behind its tail. Doors were opened, and three gang members forced a blindfolded and bound woman toward the plane.

Dante and his personal guards stormed over.

"Get her on the plane, now," the gang leader said. "Faster!" He strode over to the plane's side door and hoisted himself up. He leaned into the cockpit where the pilot was seated, checking instruments and flicking switches.

"Get the engines going," Dante ordered. "I want us in the air now."

Just as the words left his lips, he heard one of his men call out from over by the trucks. Dante turned around and jumped to the ground.

His men were looking in the distance toward a distant but rapidly approaching vehicle. It was flying through the field, heading straight toward them.

"Motherfuckers," Dante grunted. He raised his voice and added, "Take their asses down!"

He had no doubt as to who it was. Sure as hell wasn't the police. It was the two Americans. As his men took aim, Dante turned back to look at their victim. He recognized her dark flowing hair and her tall, lean body. Scarlett. The girl they were after. The one who'd already fetched an impressive sum from their black market buyer.

He looked up at the vehicle roaring toward them. He needed a little insurance, just in case. She'd do nicely.

THIRTY-FOUR

We watched as the helicopter touched down in a field far off to our left. There was a large structure beside it. A handful of vehicles. And what looked like a…

"A plane!" Ange exclaimed. "Logan, they're loading onto a plane."

My heart raced. I kept my hands gripped tight to the wheel, my foot pressing the gas pedal to the floor. But it wasn't enough. The road continued straight, then veered right. The plane was to our left. If I followed the road, we'd weave back around to reach our destination and lose precious time. Too much time. By the time we reached it, the bird would be in the air. I had no doubt of that.

I looked out the open window to my left, examining the field and countryside. It was mostly flat and devoid of obstacles.

"Hold on, Ange!"

I let off the gas. Once we coasted down to fifty miles per hour, I eased us to the left and drove with reckless abandon over the muddy shoulder and into the field. The Jeep bounced and shook over the rough ground, but I still accelerated and maintained control. We had a quarter of a mile of ground to cover, and then we needed to formulate one hell of an on-the-fly plan to take all of them out and retrieve Scarlett.

We were severely outnumbered. That much was clear. There were two trucks and a chopper. I expected no less than eight thugs in all. Each fully armed. Not to mention Dante Salazar, the leader of the gang, who had a ruthless reputation.

Ange reached behind us and grabbed the hard case from the backseat. Unclasping the hinges, she opened it and began assembling her collapsible Lapua sniper rifle. It didn't take her long to get it together and ready. Even in the fast-moving, shaking vehicle.

I kept my eyes forward. The trucks, the plane, and the guys standing between them were getting clearer in my vision.

"On my go," Ange exclaimed, "brake to a stop and give me ten seconds."

I nodded. She was already a step ahead of the game. We needed to even the odds, and she knew just the way.

"Ready," she said, adjusting her position and focusing through the windshield at our enemies. "Now!"

I let off the gas. Pressing softly on the brake, I brought our speed down to twenty, then turned the wheel to the left and we slid to a stop with the Jeep tilted to the left so that Ange was facing the action.

With her back against the seat, she raised her rifle. She stuck the barrel out the open window and pressed the butt against her shoulder. Focusing through the scope, she hovered her right index finger over the trigger as she took aim. She was like a professional musician. She knew the ins and outs of her tool of the trade blindfolded and backward. It was a smooth cycle of muscle memory actions.

Just moments after I brought the Jeep to a stop, she pressed the trigger.

A loud boom tore an ear-rattling hole in the peaceful evening air. She adjusted her aim less than an inch and fired a second time. A third shot. A fourth. Barely enough time to blink between shots.

I peered through the side of the windshield. Watched the activity over by the trucks and the plane. The gang members scrambled for cover, carefully avoiding their fallen comrades lying prone in the field courtesy of Ange.

The mental clock in my head ticked and ticked. Counting up to ten seconds. One thousand five. One thousand six.

"Shit," Ange said, lowering her rifle. "They're grabbing a female hostage for cover." She turned to me and added, "Time to step on it, Dodge."

She didn't need to tell me twice. Though it had only been seven seconds, it felt like we'd been out in the open for an eternity.

I stomped the gas pedal. The tires kicked up grass and dirt before gaining traction and accelerating us over the field. Just as we took off, the sound of automatic gunfire filled the air. Bullets whizzed by my window. A few slammed and sparked against the grille. One shattered through the windshield and nearly put a quick end to our attack.

I cut to the right, keeping my foot pressed and the engine roaring with as much power as it could muster.

I drove us parallel to the plane for a hundred yards before turning back to the left. I'd changed our approach angle, putting the large metal structure between us and the gang members.

The hailstorm of gunfire that had been relentlessly barraging our vehicle stopped.

Suddenly, the engine began billowing out black smoke. It was time to get out and take them down on foot.

The engine sputtered and rattled. Our rpms plummeted. Our speed followed.

I put us in neutral and coasted the rest of the way to the back of the building, then brought us to an abrupt stop along the back wall. In unison, we shoved our doors open and jumped out. Along with my holstered Sig and sheathed dive knife, I reached into the back and grabbed my M4 carbine assault rifle. Ange still clutched her Lapua. Her trusty Glock was holstered under the right side of her waistband. It was time to close in and finish the job.

"How many are left?" I said as we moved side by side around the back right corner of the building.

"I put down three. I'd say there's four left. Not including the pilots."

When we reached the corner, I heard footsteps running toward us. I dropped down, kept to cover, then jumped out when the figure came into view. My right hand grabbed hold of the barrel of his AK-47 and shoved it up. He managed to fire a quick spurt of gunfire before I slammed the butt of my M4 into his face and knocked him on his ass.

Three left.

We peeked around the corner, then moved in. There was no activity along the right wall of the structure. But once we reached the end, we spotted two guys kneeling beside the trucks, aiming rifles straight for us.

"In here," Ange said as we jumped back to avoid a storm of bullets.

Rounds whistled by, a few striking the metal walls as Ange grabbed hold of me and pulled me toward a rusty side door. It squealed open and we quickly surveyed the interior. It was a hangar bay. A large open and empty space with concrete floor, rows of tools, metal desks, spare parts, and a massive ladder. There were also two men standing in the middle.

They both were dressed in dirty gray coveralls. They raised their arms in the air the moment they spotted us. The wrenches they'd been holding fell from their hands. The solid metal tools rattled against the floor as we moved toward them.

They weren't angry or threatening. They just looked scared. A few stray bullets tore through the thin metal walls. We dropped to the concrete floor and moved to the other side of the hangar. We were pinned down, and we needed a plan. We needed a quick distraction.

"On my signal, open the doors," I said to the mechanics in Spanish.

They stared at me for a few seconds, terror gripping them at their core.

I repeated the order, and they nodded and stepped toward what I hoped was the door's controls.

Turning to Ange, I said, "Alright, now you—"

"Way ahead of you," she said as she stormed toward the door beside her.

I hoped that when the big doors opened, the gang members would aim toward the opening, giving Ange and me the perfect opportunity to catch them off guard on their flank.

I locked eyes with the older mechanic. I gave Ange a five-second head start to get into position, then counted down.

"*Uno…dos…tres!*"

The man pressed a button on the controls. I heard the groan of mechanical components, then the screech of metal against metal as the massive doors began to slide apart from each other.

I took off through the side door. I expected gunfire to erupt, for the gang members to take the bait, but I heard only the opening of the doors. Ange was kneeling beside the corner of the hangar, aiming toward the trucks and airplane. She wasn't firing either.

As the doors opened, they cast a bright light over the scene. I could clearly see the trucks parked behind the plane. The three remaining guys were standing. The one in the front held a girl in his arms. He also had a pistol pressed against the side of her head.

By the ever-intensifying light, Ange and I could see her perfectly.

It was Scarlett.

THIRTY-FIVE

My eyes focused in on Scarlett, looking her over from head to toe. She appeared to be alright. No visible injuries. No bloodstains. But she was scared. She was shaking, tears were streaking down her face, and she was hunched over.

She looked up. For a brief moment, we made eye contact. She mouthed something to us.

They were far off, roughly fifty yards. But that didn't matter. I knew what she was saying.

Help me.

Ange and I moved in side by side, she with her Lapua raised and me with my Sig. We quickly closed the gap. The guy holding on to Scarlett looked about my height, lean and with long black hair.

He looked familiar, and I decided that this was the relative of Benito Salazar. This was Dante, the nephew who'd decided to join in the family business.

"Not another step!" he yelled out over the sounds

of the engines and spinning propellers.

He had a thug standing beside him. Another behind him beside the open plane door. They both had rifles aimed straight at us.

Ange and I froze in place. We still had our weapons raised and locked in. Dante held Scarlett in front of him, blocking his body. We'd have a shifting target only a few inches wide if we were going to take a shot.

"Drop your weapons, now!" Dante barked.

It wasn't gonna happen. Our weapons were the only things keeping us alive. If we dropped them, there was no doubt in my mind that the two thugs with the rifles would fill us with lead seconds after they hit the ground.

"Let her go!" I yelled. "Do it now and we won't kill any of you. You can fly out of here and we won't try and stop you. Just let her go, now."

Dante gave a sinister smile and shook his head.

"You will never have her back," he stated. "You have come all this way, you have come so far only to fail now. This bitch is already sold. Business is business."

Dante forced Scarlett toward the side door of the plane. Just as they were about to reach it, Scarlett looked up again. Her expression had shifted from fear to intense rage. In an instant, she yelled out wildly.

She grabbed hold of Dante's arm with both hands, bent her knees, then snapped her hips back and rolled him over the top of her. Dante was so caught off guard by the attack that he had no choice but to go along for the ride as Scarlett slammed him hard onto the grass.

Ange and I wasted no time. The moment Dante's gun was forced from Scarlett's head, we fired a

241

succession of well-placed rounds into the thug right beside them. The rounds struck through his body and sent them down hard.

The moment his bloodied body hit the grass, the guy back by the door opened fire. A stream of automatic gunfire screamed toward us, forcing us to dive behind the nearest truck for cover. Bullets pounded the metal and glass, shooting sparks into the night air.

We kept low, our bodies pressed flat to the grass. I rolled left. Ange rolled right. Just as we peeked around, the plane's engine groaned louder and the propellers picked up speed. Dante was back on his feet and forcing Scarlett through the plane's open door.

The big guy was right at his side, his aim still directed toward the truck we were taking cover behind. He fired again, pelting the grass and tires and dirt around us. We wanted to retaliate, but Scarlett was too close. The last thing we wanted was for a stray bullet to catch her and put a tragic end to the entire thing.

Dante climbed in first, the big guy right behind him. Using Scarlett as a shield, they carried her up, then pulled her out of our view just as the plane began to accelerate.

I rolled around the corner of the truck, jumped to my feet, and took off in a full sprint toward the plane. With the only men still standing out of sight inside the plane, I kept my Sig lowered and pumped my arms. My left leg hurt like hell from being struck by the pellet earlier that day, but I ignored it and forced my body to move as fast as it could.

The plane picked up speed rapidly, but I managed to reach the side door just as the big guy was trying to manhandle it shut. He glanced back at me, his big eyes bulging. Maybe he'd thought we wouldn't catch up. Maybe he'd thought we'd been struck.

Wrong on both accounts.

I dove, launching my body through the air, and slammed a right fist across his jaw. His head jerked sideways and he grunted. Not a knockout blow, but enough to get him out from the entryway.

I slammed hard into the edge of the opening, my upper body inside and my feet just a few inches off the grass. Grabbing hold of a metal seat leg off to my right, I hoisted myself up into the cabin.

The big guy recovered from the blow just as I came to my feet. He yelled out and lunged toward me. In my peripherals, I spotted movement to my right. It was Dante. He had one hand gripping tight to Scarlett's hair while the other raised a Browning Hi-Power pistol straight at me. They were just a few rows back and moving down the aisle toward me.

Just as the big guy threw a meaty fist at me, I sprang toward him and slammed my forehead square into his nose. The fragile bones cracked and blood flowed out as he yelled in pain and rage.

As Dante aimed his pistol at me, I grabbed the guy by his vest collar, pulled him in front of me, and dropped down. Two rounds exploded from the chamber like cracks of angry lightning in the small cabin. The bullets tore into his vest just as I hit the deck.

With my right hand still gripping my Sig, I took aim under the two seats beside me. Dante was keeping Scarlett in front of him, but his legs were easy targets. I pulled the trigger, sending a round into his left shin. The bone splintered and the leg flew out from under him. He fell hard, nearly knocked unconscious as his forehead hit an armrest and he tumbled to the aisle.

I was just about to redirect my aim and fire off a second round, this one through his forehead, when the big guy intervened. He'd recovered from the blows to his vest and slammed his massive boot down onto my hand, sending excruciating pain crawling up my arm and causing me to let go of my Sig.

As I turned around to engage the big guy, he dropped down and punched me hard in the chest. I tried to retaliate, but he was much bigger and stronger than I was. And he had me pinned down.

He yelled and wrapped his massive hands around my neck. His muscular fingers dug in and I heard a terrifying crunching sound. I clawed at him with my good hand. Tried to gouge his eyes. To bite his hands. Anything.

Just as my vision began to blur, I heard a thump to my left. I could barely see Ange holding onto the side of the plane. Somehow, she'd managed to grab hold of the speeding plane and pull herself up.

She aimed her Glock straight at the big guy.

He glanced at her, loosened his grip, then dove toward her.

Ange fired two quick shots.

The big guy's head exploded and he collapsed into her. I gagged for precious air and rubbed my eyes. Rolling over, I crawled to the door and peeked out. There was no sign of either Ange or the big guy.

The cabin shook as the plane picked up speed. We were about to take off. I could feel it. Could feel the powerful gusts of wind gushing in through the side door.

Ange is fine, I told myself. *The big guy's dead. She'll be banged up from the fall, but she's a tough girl. As tough as they come.*

My mind shifted to Scarlett, and Dante.

I sprang to my feet and darted toward the aisle. Dante was still on the ground, clutching his bleeding leg with one hand and scrambling for his pistol with the other. Scarlett kicked Dante's gun away. She turned and strode into my arms, her body shaking in fear, tears streaking down her face. I squeezed her tight.

Peeking over my shoulder, I saw the dark field passing by in a blur through the open side door.

We're moving way too fast to jump for it.

Less than a second later, I felt my stomach sink as the plane angled back.

The plane jerked, throwing both of us into the closest seat as the angle shifted back even more.

I struggled to my feet.

"Stay here," I said to Scarlett.

Grabbing the tops of the seats for support, I moved back a few rows to where Dante was lying on his back. Blood soaked his right pant leg. He wailed and gripped the wound. His body was shaking, his eyes filled with rage.

I put him out of his misery with a strong kick across the side of his face. His head jerked. His body went motionless, curled up at the base of the seat beside him.

"Logan!" Scarlett screamed suddenly.

I looked up. The cockpit door was opening.

I moved as fast as I could down the aisle, then darted for the cockpit door just as one of the pilots appeared. He looked pissed off and was holding a subcompact pistol in both hands.

He stared me down, but just before he was able to aim his handgun around the door, I jumped and slammed my left shoulder into the door.

The heavy metal door slammed into the pilot. He groaned and fired off a few sporadic rounds into the overhead.

I grabbed hold of his wrist and held it up as he kicked the door back open. It nearly knocked me down, but I regained my balance and forced him back into the cockpit.

With his finger still on the trigger, he fired a few more rounds as I struggled to knock the gun from his grasp. A handful of bullets tore through the controls, shooting up sparks, causing the panels to smoke and blink and annoying alarms to go off.

The gun finally rattled from his hands as we fell to the floor between the two seats. As fast as I could, I reached behind me with my left hand, grabbed my dive knife, and stabbed it through the pilot's heart.

The copilot suddenly let go of his yoke. The plane leveled out from its previous incline, nearly causing me to topple forward into the damaged controls. He yelled something in Spanish that I didn't understand, then lunged for the dropped weapon.

He was short and skinny, and he clearly lacked fighting experience. It was a good thing. My right hand was nearly useless and my body ached.

I grabbed him by his shirt collar and slammed his head into the seat behind him. He went out like a light and slid down in his seat.

With all my assailants down, I was tempted to take a few seconds to catch my breath. But I didn't have a few seconds. With the damaged controls and with no one holding the yoke, the plane was already starting to shake.

I leaned over the copilot and found the switch for the autopilot. It didn't work. The nose continued to slowly dip down.

I heard footsteps behind me. I glanced back and saw Scarlett appear in the narrow doorway.

"What's going on?" she asked.

Her mouth dropped when she looked at the two guys. One was soaked in blood, the other unconscious.

"We got a bit of a problem," I said, trying my best to control the plane.

The sparks caused a small fire to burn under the paneling. Smoke filled the cockpit. I tried the throttles and even they wouldn't work anymore. We were dead in the sky, soaring in a bird that didn't want to fly anymore.

"I thought you were a pilot," she yelled.

"I am. But this plane's going down. The controls are all shot up to hell."

I tried my best to stabilize us, but it was no use. We were angling down and there was no stopping it now.

I turned around and started opening gear lockers like a madman.

"What are you doing?" Scarlett asked.

"Parachutes," I said. "We're gonna need to jump."

"Did you say jump?"

I ignored her while rapidly slamming open and peering into lockers. No dice. I moved out of the cockpit and checked an overhead compartment. Bingo. A row of parachutes.

I grabbed two of them and strapped the first onto Scarlett, who was looking at me like I was crazy.

"I've never skydived before," she said.

"Well, this is your first lesson."

I gave her as extensive a tutorial as time would permit, then strapped the second one onto my back.

247

"Jump out as far as you can," I said. "And you're gonna have to pull the chute quick. We're only a few thousand feet up."

She stared with frightened eyes out the open door. The wind was blowing in violently, the damaged plane swaying back and forth and angling downward in the pitch darkness.

"Hey," I said, grabbing her hand. I pulled her close and wrapped my arms around her. "It's going to be okay. You can do this, Scarlett."

I looked her in the eyes, then told her again that she could do this. She nodded and brushed the loose hairs from her face.

I held on to her and we inched toward the open door. With one hand gripping the back of her harness and the other the door frame, she stayed right at the edge.

"Wait for the roll," I said. "We don't want to get hit by the tail."

I timed the movements of the plane as best I could. My mental clock ticked down dangerously. We had precious little time before the plane would crash into the ocean.

"Alright, on three we jump," I yelled over the howling wind. I timed the plane, waited for us to tilt toward the right. "One…two…three!"

Just as I let go of Scarlett's harness, a hand grabbed me hard from behind and pulled me back. Scarlett was already falling forward. There was no stopping her momentum, and she was just out of my reach. She looked back with petrified eyes just as she flew out of the door. She vanished into the windswept night air in an instant.

I jerked my body around and saw Dante. He'd

248

staggered to his feet and was holding tight to my pack with one hand while his other gripped a switchblade.

"You son of a bitch," he snarled, staring me down with the eyes of a rabid beast.

He stabbed the long narrow blade straight toward me. Just as the tip was about to bite viciously into my flesh, I grabbed his forearm. He yelled and fought to press it harder toward me. I yelled and fought to press it harder away. For what felt like an eternity, but was only a second or two, the blade shook just inches away from my chest.

With the plane tilting dangerously forward, it was clear that this was do or die. Whether I took Dante down or not, we'd both be dead soon regardless.

I yelled, slammed my forehead into his face, then jerked his hands down. As he wailed, I managed to twist the blade 180 degrees and pressed with all my remaining strength. The blade stabbed through Dante's body, just under his right collarbone.

He yelled louder, fiercer, all of his rage boiling over.

I buried the blade deeper, until the tip protruded out his back, then knocked him across the face again.

"Before you die, know this," I yelled, holding his limp body up and keeping the blade lodged. "I killed your uncle. I killed Benito Salazar."

I let go and took a shaky step backward. Stabilizing myself, I jumped and kicked him across the cabin. The force launched my body backward and I flew out the open side door. Tucking my body, I flew into the loud roaring haze of the night and felt a strong whiplash as the plane's tail rocketed right past me.

I spun wildly. A dark frenzy. I couldn't see anything. Couldn't tell up from down.

I felt myself losing consciousness but forced my mind and body to stay alert.

You're low, Dodge. You've got… to… open… the…

In the chaotic freefalling spin, my right hand found the ripcord. With the air howling around me and the dark ocean getting closer and closer, I grabbed it tight and jerked it away from me.

THIRTY-SIX

Jack Rubio stood on the bow of the decrepit-looking trawler. He held a pair of binoculars up to his eyes and scanned over the northwestern shores of Cuba.

The scene was mostly dark. A few distant flickering lights here and there. Hotels, houses, a few restaurants maybe. There was also a handful of distant fishing boats, most heading in after a long day.

"No sign of a freighter, boy," he said, petting Atticus with his free hand.

The Lab sat patiently, every sound and smell causing his head to swivel back and forth.

Jack performed another scan of the horizon, then lowered the binos and glanced at his dive watch. It had been forty-five minutes since Logan had called. The trip over had been quick, and he'd been idle for fifteen.

Jack stretched, then sat beside Atticus, his back against the front of the pilothouse.

He didn't mind waiting. He loved the ocean. Everything about it. He could sit and stare out over the water for hours, letting his mind drift with the current. The fresh sea air, the lapping waves against the hull, the sound of the wind. He'd always considered himself a simple man. A boat, the ocean, a good cup of coffee. Anything beyond that was just a bonus.

He rose to his feet and took another look-see. Nothing out of the ordinary.

He headed inside, refilled his mug with coffee, then plopped down in the cockpit. He switched on the radar and leaned back into the cushioned seat. Though an eyesore, it amazed Jack how fancy the trawler's electronics were. Top-of-the-line from the sonar to the coffeemaker. Easily costing the original owner more than his entire boat.

He took a sip of coffee and glanced at his watch again.

Where are you, bro? he thought.

He grabbed his phone from the dash. Nothing. No missed calls or messages.

Just as he slid the phone into his boardshorts pocket, Atticus stirred. He lifted his head and stared out the port side of the windscreen.

"What is it, boy?" Jack said, leaning forward in the seat.

The Lab was listening intently, his gaze zeroed in and focused. Most of the side windows were cracked open. Jack switched off the radar and listened as well.

It took a few seconds, but he soon heard a distant humming noise.

He set his mug on the dash, grabbed the binoculars, and headed back out onto the bow. Atticus jumped to the deck and followed right beside him.

The humming sound grew louder and more distinct. After years on the water, Jack's ears were incredibly sensitive. He could differentiate the different brands and horsepower of engines from miles away. He didn't even need to see it to know that what he was hearing wasn't a boat at all. It was a plane. A plane engine and rotors slicing through the air far in the dark distance.

He stepped up to the edge of the bow alongside Atticus and directed his gaze toward the sound. He spotted the flashing white lights far in the distance. The plane was flying low, just a few thousand feet, and was on a northwest trajectory, sweeping out over the ocean.

Jack watched the plane intently. There was something off about it. Not only was it flying too low, but it was shaking. Like there was a mechanical issue of some kind.

There clearly weren't any airports nearby. He hadn't seen any other planes on the horizon since he'd arrived.

He lowered the binos but kept his eyes on the plane. Atticus stood beside him and barked.

"Yeah, something's wrong, boy. I feel it too."

He was just about to head back into the cockpit to call in the mysterious aircraft to authorities when the plane took a sudden turn. It angled side to side, then shifted its nose downward. Jack wasn't an airplane guy, but it didn't take one to see that the plane would crash into the ocean within a minute if it maintained its speed and suicidal angle.

He sprinted into the cockpit and fired up the engines. Keeping his eyes glued on the distant aircraft, he hit the throttles and quickly brought the trawler up to forty knots. A smooth tilt of the helm put them on a direct course for where Jack was certain the plane would crash if its pilot didn't do something drastic soon.

He watched as the shaking craft flew closer and closer to the water below. Suddenly, he spotted something. A solid black figure set against the evening sky. After just a few seconds, he realized what it was.

A parachute. Somebody just ditched.

He shifted his course. Taking the wind into account as well as the jumper's angle, he predicted where they would land.

An open chute slows a freefalling person's speed to roughly seventeen miles per hour. The person had jumped from fifteen hundred feet up, meaning they'd reach the ocean in just under a minute.

Jack closed the distance as much as he could in that time and watched as the silhouette of the jumper splashed into the water. The chute followed, blown by the wind and spread over the sea just beyond them.

Jack eased back on the throttles, brought the jumper right off the port bow. Stepping out and peeking over the gunwale, he realized that it was a girl. He stepped back to the helm, idled the engines, then stepped out and tossed her a life ring.

She grabbed hold of it and he pulled the rope, reeling her in. When she was within twenty feet, Jack realized who she was by the light of the moon.

"Holy crap, Scarlett?" he gasped, his mouth agape.

She coughed up a mouthful of seawater and nodded. He pulled her to the stern, then reached down and grabbed hold of her harness. She pulled herself up as well and managed to reach the top of the transom and slide down onto the deck. Jack went to work on the harness, unclipping it and securing it to a rod holder.

"Are you alright?" he said, looking her over.

She was shaking, her eyes big, but she didn't appear to be injured.

"Where's Logan?" she said, her voice filled with desperation. "Where is he?"

Jack shook his head. How the heck would he know? He hadn't seen his friend since earlier that afternoon.

He was just about to ask what had happened when a second splash filled the evening air. It was far off and came in the direction the plane had flown.

Scarlett struggled to her feet and stepped toward the starboard gunwale. Jack followed right behind.

"That's him," she gasped. "That has to be him."

They were too far away to see anything but the distant collapsing parachute over the surface of the water. Jack turned and darted for the harness still resting against the transom. He quickly pulled up the chute, Scarlett helping, then dropped it in a pile on the deck.

He moved into the cockpit, fired up the engines, and motored toward the second jumper. He grabbed his compact Desert Eagle and slid it into the small of his back, just in case it wasn't his friend.

Jack slowed as he reached the figure in the water. He grabbed a powerful flashlight, stepped out, and shined it toward the second jumper. A smile came over his face. It was Logan. He was treading water and giving Jack a left-handed thumbs-up.

THIRTY-SEVEN

My chute opened with a forceful yank of the ripcord. It unraveled, quickly caught the wind, and jerked me to a near stop. I'd been spinning frantically upon exiting the plane, and the whiplash nearly knocked me out. My mind was in a haze as I soared through the dark tropical air.

Less than ten seconds after the chute deployed, I splashed hard into the water. The ocean overtook me, blanketing me in a veil of warm water. I sank like a rock, then kicked for the surface, careful not to get tangled in the risers and rigging lines.

Breaking the surface, I exhaled and took in a few deep breaths of air. I was in pain, aching, and weary, but breathing. Somehow I'd managed to scrape out of the mess with my life.

I looked straight up, then down at my floating parachute. If I'd pulled the cord a fraction of a second later, my splash landing would've been a much different and more painful story. I could've easily ended up paralyzed or dead.

I looked off to the northwest. The plane was angling downward sharper and sharper. It was a black speck on the horizon, its flashing lights nearly all I could see.

Suddenly, the darkness around me was illuminated by a solid beam of bright light. I shielded my eyes. My mind raced back to the last time I'd been strobed at night out on the water. Forty-eight hours earlier in the Gulf. The freighter. The night the whole shitstorm had begun.

Thankfully, it wasn't a freighter and it wasn't an enemy.

My eyes adjusted. The outline of a familiar boat came into view. The mental clarity was followed right after by the recognition of a figure standing along the starboard railing and aiming the light at me.

It was Jack.

I raised my left hand out of the water and gave him a thumbs-up.

Then the smile on my face somehow managed to get even bigger. Stepping up toward him along the rail, I spotted a second figure. It was Scarlett. She was alive and well.

She waved, and I waved back as Jack stepped into the cockpit and accelerated the trawler my way. I unclipped the harness with my left hand, my right throbbing in pain as my adrenaline wore off.

Jack motored the trawler right beside me and I grabbed hold of the stern with my left hand.

"Holy shit, bro," Jack said, idling the engine and stepping out toward the stern. "Are you alright?"

"Never better," I said, my words shaky and rushed. "Give me a hand, will you? I'm down one."

Leaning over, they both helped me over and I flopped onto the dock, soaked, in pain, and weary.

Atticus barked, ran over and licked my face. Scarlett jumped into my arms. She hugged me tight and buried her face into my chest. I patted the back of her head.

"It's alright," I said. "Everything's going to be alright. It's all over now."

She couldn't talk. She could barely breathe she was so emotional. Her reaction was more than understandable given what she'd experienced. A traumatizing ordeal. A painful wound that I hoped, with time, would heal.

We sat embracing with my back against the transom while Jack pulled my harness up out of the water and gathered my chute. I heard a distant grumble from far out over the horizon. I directed my gaze over the starboard bow. The distant flashes of lights from the plane were no longer visible. The plane had crashed. Dante was dead. It was all over.

I wonder if the sharks will enjoy the taste of him as much as they had his uncle. Whatever's left of his body after the crash anyway.

When Jack finished, he looked down at us.

"I gotta tell ya, bro," he said, "when you told me to stand by at this location, I didn't expect to see you two parachuting out of a crashing plane."

He patted me on the back, then turned and headed into the cockpit to mark the position of the downed plane on the GPS.

Scarlett's breathing slowed a little. She loosened her grip, then pulled herself back a few inches and looked me in the eyes.

"Thank you, Logan," she said. Her eyes were filled with tears, her voice soft and innocent. "Thank you for coming for me."

I smiled, doing my best to ignore the pain in my hand, shoulder, and leg.

"We didn't think twice about it," I said. "That was a nice move, by the way. Dante didn't know what hit him."

She grinned. "Well, I learned from the best."

Jack stepped out of the cockpit holding his sat phone. He walked over and handed it to me.

"I'm sure Ange is worried sick," he said.

I quickly dialed her number. She picked up on the second ring.

"Jack, where are you?" Ange said frantically. "Did you see a pl—"

"Ange, it's me," I said.

"Logan? Oh, God, are you alright?"

"Just fine. I'm on the trawler with Jack. And there's someone else here who'd like to talk to you."

I handed the phone to Scarlett. More tears. More struggled words. They were both relieved and happy beyond comprehension.

I leaned back against the transom and listened to them talk, my mouth unable to keep from smiling. Looking up at the big night sky, I took in a deep satisfying breath and let it out.

THIRTY-EIGHT

Cayo Jutias, Cuba

I woke up naturally to the sound of waves lapping against the shore and palm leaves rustling in the breeze. I opened my eyes, blinked a few times.

I was lying in a queen-sized bed with a white comforter. Ange lay beside me, her head resting on a pillow. Her face was angelic in the morning glow from the nearby open window.

I kissed her forehead, then swung off the bed and planted my bare feet on the wood floor. Not wanting to wake her, I tiptoed into the living room then out the creaky front door.

My soul smiled as I moved down the faded wooden steps and onto the fine warm sand. My body ached all over. I'd taken a number of solid punches over the past twenty-four hours. Not to mention a pellet to the leg and a stomping boot to the hand. But

I'd been banged and battered more than my share of times over the years, and I always managed to bounce back. The human body is an incredible thing. It's great at healing itself if given proper time, care, and treatment.

I sauntered across the beach, heading for the surf. When the clear, warm water covered my feet, I looked out and took in a deep breath. It was nearly noon, the sun high overhead. And it was probably nearing ninety degrees, but the ocean breeze made it perfect.

I bent down and splashed some seawater on my face with my left hand. My right index and middle fingers had been fractured by the thug's stomping boot and were wrapped in splints.

With the water dripping down my face, I rose and directed my gaze left, then right. Palm trees hugged the shoreline about a quarter of a mile in each direction. In between the surf and foliage was as beautiful a beach as could be found anywhere. A white sandy paradise with crystal clear waters lapping the shoreline, transitioning to turquoise and then dark blue on the horizon.

The only break came in the form of a long, skinny dock just a hundred yards to my left. The trawler was tied off at the end.

It was Heaven on earth. And I had it all to myself. There wasn't another soul as far as the eye could see.

The retreating waves buried my stoic feet in the wet sand. I pulled them free one at a time, then turned around and looked toward the place we'd spent the night. It was simple. A yellow-painted two-bedroom beach cottage with a thatched roof, a small porch, and hammock. No more than seven hundred square feet. Unassuming and off the beaten path.

I closed my eyes and thought back to the previous evening. After the final encounter with Dante Salazar and his gang, and after giving Scarlett her first spur-of-the-moment skydiving lesson, I'd contacted Sanchez via my sat phone. After I'd informed her of what all had happened, she'd directed us to meet her at a dock on Cayo Jutias, an island just a few miles northwest of Santa Lucía.

It was after we'd met with her that she'd offered us a place to stay in one of the government's safe houses. We'd all happily obliged. Arriving so late, we'd spent half an hour hugging and catching up before fatigue overtook us. We'd all crashed moments after switching off the lights. It had been dark, and we'd been so spent that we hadn't realized that she'd put us up in a gorgeous haven.

I walked along the shore, letting my mind wander and getting my blood flowing, my own form of carnal meditation. After traversing the beach from end to end, I made my way back to the cottage.

Just as I reached the porch, I heard a car pull up and headed around to the driveway. I passed by a small shed and spotted a few beach chairs and colorful kayaks through the cracks in the wood.

Out front, a white sedan pulled into view. It had a blue strobe light on its roof and a Cuban police emblem on the front two doors. It parked alongside a 1950s Chevy truck that had been commandeered from Dante and his thugs by Ange the previous evening after they shot up the Jeep's engine. The driver's side door of the sedan opened and Sanchez stepped out.

She was wearing her white button-up, black pants, and dark sunglasses. A second officer dressed in full uniform, who I recognized from the previous evening, stepped out from the passenger side and leaned

262

against the car while Sanchez strode toward me.

"Glad I didn't wake you," she said. "Figured I'd give you all some time to recuperate after the day you had yesterday."

I smiled faintly, then motioned toward the house.

"Thank you," I said. "The place is perfect."

"It's the least we could do."

Sanchez motioned toward the other officer, who grabbed two large bags from the back of the car. Walking over, he set them in the shade of a palm tree beside me. Sanchez told me that it was Ange's and my dive gear. We'd told them where it was the previous evening and they'd tracked it down on the sailboat.

I thanked her and we stood in silence for a few seconds. Then her phone buzzed, she checked the screen, then slid it back into her pocket.

"So, what happens now?" I said.

"With Dante out of the picture, and with the dent you guys made, the western faction of the gang will likely die off. And the eastern... well, we're working on it."

"That's good to hear. But it's not exactly what I meant."

She glanced over her shoulder at the other officer, then looked back at me. Her lips formed the closest thing I imagined they ever did to a smile.

"No, I didn't think so," she said. "When it comes to you and your wife, I'd just as soon leave your involvement off the record. If that's alright with you."

I was taken aback by her words. I'd fully expected to be neck-deep in interviews, statements, and government red tape for at least a few weeks. After all, we'd entered the country illegally and had racked up a significant body count.

"So, that's it, then?" I said, raising my eyebrows.

She nodded. "That's it."

She extended her right hand. Glancing down and remembering that mine was bandaged up, she switched to her left, and we shook.

"Thanks again," she said. "I guess I may have misjudged you. We may have differing strategies, you and I, but I have to admit that you two did a good job here."

I thanked her as well. She sure didn't have to go to such lengths to get us off the hook.

She glanced at the cottage, then back at me.

"The fridge and pantry are both stocked," she said. "Feel free to stay the week, Dodge. It's the least I can do." She motioned toward the parked Chevy and added, "This truck's yours as long as you like. Just leave it here whenever you leave. And don't worry about your jeep rental. We'll take care of the damage."

She turned, walked back to her squad car, and opened the driver's-side door. Before getting in, she said, "You two were never here. Got that?"

I nodded.

"And don't let your experiences yesterday paint Cuba in too negative a light," she added. "I love my country. It is full of beautiful places and beautiful people. I wouldn't think of living anywhere else."

I waved as she climbed in, started the engine, and drove out of sight down the sandy road.

THIRTY-NINE

I picked up the bags of dive gear, turned around, and headed for the cottage. I froze when I spotted Ange standing in front of the open front door. Her ninja-like stealth abilities never ceased to amaze me.

"I heard the car pull up," she said. "What's the deal? They chucking us into Guantanamo?"

I chuckled.

She moved down to the bottom step, and I met her there, our heights evened out.

"Looks like we're in the clear."

We smiled at each other, kissed, then I dropped the gear and we hugged. Her body felt good pressed against mine.

I heard shuffling feet and watched Atticus trot into view. Even he'd slept more than usual, but he jumped with enthusiasm when he met us at the porch. While hugging Ange, I reached around and petted my fun-loving pooch.

I loosened my grip on Ange and said, "Hungry?"

"Starving."

After stowing the gear, we migrated to the kitchen. Sanchez hadn't been kidding. The place was freshly stocked with everything we needed, and there was enough to last well over a week.

We cooked up some granola-banana pancakes, bacon, and scrambled eggs and started up the coffeemaker. The smell caused even the heavy-sleeping Jack to stir on the living room couch.

Halfway through eating, Jack looked out one of the ocean-facing windows and said, "So, what's the plan for today?"

I answered without hesitating. "I spotted a few beach chairs in a shed beside the cottage."

My beach bum friend smiled and took another massive bite of syrup-drenched pancake.

"I think he approves," Ange said with a big grin.

After eating, we cleaned up, then dragged out the beach chairs and umbrellas and filled a cooler with ice and drinks. It was a perfect day. A slight breeze and just a few scattered clouds from horizon to horizon.

Scarlett woke up and stepped down onto the sand an hour later. She squinted and rubbed her eyes as she walked toward us. She'd showered and changed into the extra clothes in the closet and was wearing black shorts and a white tank top.

She looked good. And she looked even better after eating leftover breakfast to her heart's content and spending the afternoon relaxing in our own private paradise.

We swam, kayaked, and lounged in the sun until the sun sank into the ocean. While watching the natural evening spectacle, Ange and I curled up on one of the beach chairs. We stared in awe as the sky transitioned from vibrant yellows up high to deep oranges near the horizon, the distant glowing orb sending a blanket of streaking light that sparkled over the surface of the water.

I kissed Ange on the forehead, then smiled at her.

"What?" she said softly, not needing to look away from the view to see that there was something on my mind.

"Remember a few nights ago when we were listening to the Wayward Suns at Conch Haven?"

"Tough to forget," she giggled.

"You'd mentioned that we were due for a trip."

I looked up and down at the long beach surrounding us. Glanced at Scarlett, who was playing with Atticus in the sand. Spotted Jack walking toward us from up the beach, carrying a sack of coconuts in one hand and a machete in the other.

"This count?" I added.

She smiled, turned and kissed me.

"I'd say that it does."

We spent two more days at the secret middle-of-nowhere beach cottage. We spent our time hanging out at the beach, kayaking, snorkeling in a nearby cove, and relaxing under the tropical sun.

By the morning of the third day, we knew that it was time for us to leave. Jack missed his nephew and Lauren, who'd been looking after the seventeen-year-old while he was gone. Ange and I were excited to be back home and in the States. And most importantly, Scarlett's case manager had been calling us every day for a status update on when we'd have her back. We'd told her that she'd run into some trouble abroad and that we were handling it but left out all the specifics.

We cleaned up the cottage, tidied up the grounds, then climbed aboard the trawler. We plotted the straightforward two-hundred-mile jump across the Straits of Florida back to Key West. After a quick call to Sanchez to let her know we were leaving, Jack started up the engines and we cast off. He had us rumbling out to sea within minutes, and I watched as our temporary beach paradise grew smaller in the distance. It was bittersweet.

All good things must come to an end, I thought.

Then I turned and shifted my gaze forward at Ange and Scarlett, who were laughing up on the bow with Atticus.

Some are simply replaced by other good things.

EPILOGUE

It felt good to be home. Back to our anything but usual "routine." Back to days out on the water, morning workouts, fresh seafood, and nights on the town.

After returning from Cuba, we'd spent one more day with Scarlett before calling her children's group home in Miami. She hadn't exactly been ecstatic about having to go back, and it was hard to see her go. We'd formed a strong bond in the short time we'd known her. She was a special girl, and Ange and I both decided that we wanted to pursue adoption.

It's a long process. We were informed by Scarlett's counselor that it usually takes around a year for a prospective parent to jump through all the hoops. A ten-week preparation course, background checks, home studies and various other mandatory training.

In the meantime, Ange and I made the trip to see

her in Miami every few weeks and spoke to her on the phone every other day. The more we met with her and talked with her, the more we wanted to make her part of our little family. Ange and I both believed she'd make a great addition, and more importantly, that we could make a positive impact on her final few years before becoming an adult.

Two days after we arrived back in the Keys, Scott met us for dinner at Salty Pete's. Before we'd gotten our appetizers, he asked if he could speak with me in private.

We headed through the second-story sliding glass door, past the rows of exhibits, and into Pete's office. Scott shut the door behind us.

He stood right in front of the door, facing me. He looked to be mulling something over. He was wearing his work clothes. Black pants, nice shoes, white dress shirt, red tie. The only thing missing was his jacket.

"That was a good thing you both did," he said finally. "Really."

I shook my head.

"Scottie, you didn't pull me aside to commend me. We've never walked on eggshells before. No need to start now."

He nodded. "Look, this shit in Cuba was just scratching the surface." He stepped toward me and lowered his voice. "This is a global sex-trafficking operation. We're talking thousands of women every month. Dante and his gang were just a small part of a much bigger picture."

I looked away from him, wrapping my head around what he was saying. I knew that he was right. The large-scale magnitude of the operation had been evident early on. Ever since the cargo ship. Ever since...

"Wake," I said.

Scott nodded. "At some point, he has to be brought to justice. It's the only way this will ever be over. He's the head of this highly venomous snake. One way or another, Richard Wake has to go down."

"It's not gonna happen within the confines of the law. He's too powerful. Has too many people in his pocket."

"I know," Scott said. "To be honest, I'm surprised he hasn't come after you yet."

I was surprised as well. First, we'd stopped his corrupt oil drilling scheme in its tracks. Then we'd taken down one of his partners, Carson Richmond. Then we'd put an end to Dante and his squad. Not devastating blows to a bigshot like Wake, but certainly major jabs to his profits, not to mention his ego.

"Please tell me there's some kind of plan to take him down," I added.

"I'm working with Wilson and a few others on it."

I knew Scott had something in the works, despite the possible repercussions. If Wake found out there was a plan forming against him, he'd kill those at the top. Even a sitting senator.

"Just watch your back, Logan," he said. "I'm sensing that something's gonna happen soon. Something big."

I didn't take Scott's words lightly. He wouldn't say something like that if he didn't believe that it was true. Plus, I had the same feeling myself. Something was coming. After years of throwing myself into danger, I'd developed a sort of sixth sense to see it coming. Like the distant grumbles that foreshadow an impending storm.

Ange and I did watch our backs. But we weren't

about to let possible approaching danger keep us from living our lives.

Wait and hope.

I reminded myself of those words daily. The final words spoken by Edmond Dantès in one of my favorite books.

We went out on the water. We fished. We swam. We explored. We cooked new foods, and visited new places, and met new people all over the islands.

In early September, Scarlett and her counselor met us in Key Largo for the annual Upper Keys Lionfish Derby. From sunup to sundown, we scoured every underwater nook and cranny we could find, spearing the colorful invasive species for the good of the ecosystem.

At the end of the day, everyone gathered beside rows of barbeques and tables to carefully filet and grill the fruits of our labors. Enjoying a wild thrill, savoring tasty seafood, and saving the environment all at the same time is one hell of a way to spend an afternoon.

We said our goodbyes to Scarlett and her counselor, then hopped aboard the Baia and headed back to Key West. I engaged the autopilot, whipped up a few mojitos, and met Ange up on the bow.

We drank and smiled and kissed and laughed.

There could very well be a storm on the horizon. A wave of danger surging our way. But after a day on the water, after seeing the joyful look in Ange's eyes, and after pulling her warm body close while we watched the sunset, I felt nothing but pure happiness.

Wait and hope.

THE END

LOGAN DODGE ADVENTURES

Gold in the Keys
Hunted in the Keys
Revenge in the Keys
Betrayed in the Keys
Redemption in the Keys
Corruption in the Keys
Predator in the Keys
Legend in the Keys
Abducted in the Keys

Join the Adventure!
Sign up for my newsletter to receive updates on
upcoming books on my website:

matthewrief.com

About the Author

Matthew has a deep-rooted love for adventure and the ocean. He loves traveling, diving, rock climbing and writing adventure novels. Though he grew up in the Pacific Northwest, he currently lives in Virginia Beach with his wife, Jenny.

Made in United States
Troutdale, OR
02/13/2025

28962153R00170